Henrik Ibsen's A D

Adapted by Nicholas Mic

Henrik Ibsen's A Doll's House, Adapted by Nicholas Michael Bashour, first published in this adaptation in 2021

© Nicholas Michael Bashour 2021

Nicholas Michael Bashour has asserted his right to be identified as the author of this work. All rights reserved. No part of this publication may be reproduced or transmitted in any form or by any means, electronic or mechanical, including photocopying, recording, or any information storage or retrieval system, without prior permission in writing from the author.

Professionals and amateurs are hereby warned that this material, being fully protected under the Copyright Laws of the United States of America and all other countries of the Berne and Universal Copyright Conventions, is subject to a royalty. The author reserves the right to grant performance and other rights to non-profit educational and amateur organizations for minimal royalty fees. All rights, including but not limited to, professional, amateur, recording, motion picture, recitation, lecturing, public reading, radio and television broadcasting, and the rights of translation into foreign languages are expressly reserved.

All rights whatsoever in this play are strictly reserved. Requests to reproduce the text in whole or in part should be addressed to Nicholas Michael Bashour. Application for performance etc. by professionals or amateurs in any medium and in any language throughout the world should be made in writing before rehearsals begin to Nicholas Michael Bashour, 1830 I St NE #4, Washington DC, 20002, licensing@nicholasbashour.com. No responsibility for loss caused to any individual or organization acting on or refraining from action as a result of the material in this publication can be accepted by the author.

No performance may be given unless a license has been obtained.

Contents

Introduction i
ACT I 1
ACT II 44
ACT III 79

Introduction

Adaptor's notes:
If this is your first time reading *A Doll's House* and want to experience all of its twists and turns as they happen, you can choose to save reading the below notes and character descriptions to the end to avoid any spoilers.

While this is more of an adaptation than a translation, Henrik Ibsen wrote that "I consider it most important that the dialogue in the translations be kept as close to ordinary, everyday speech as possible...I believe that a translator should employ the style which the original author would have used if he had written in the language of those who are to read him in translation." This adaptation honors Ibsen's original dialogue and intentions (many of which had been lost in translation) while also making the dialogue sound like it was meant for actors today instead of the Victorian-era. The actors should thus seek to make the characters speak as naturally as possible (except in certain circumstances, such as Nora's affectations when "performing" for Torvald or Rank), so that they may sound very much like "ordinary, everyday" people.

Keep in mind that Ibsen had always intended for this play to be set in the present, not the past. How can we do that when the circumstances of the play are so rooted in the time in which the play was written? We can't set it in the present day because the characters wouldn't behave this way in the present. However, if we set the language in the present day while keeping everything else in the past, the circumstances of the play will work while also feeling like it belongs "in the present."

The porter character has been written out. The three Helmer children are depicted but need not be portrayed by actors. Be creative, but not silly, with how they're represented on stage. The significance of those moments is to show Nora's affection for and devotion to her children. This makes her decision to leave them all the more difficult in the end. When she tells Torvald that she doesn't want to see them before she leaves, it's because she loves them so much that if she were to see them, she would not have been able to leave.

While Ibsen himself, and different translations, have not assigned any ages to the characters, after extensive research, I've chosen to assign specific ages/ranges to them. Those ranges are significantly important to the dynamics of this play and to the way the characters behave, react to, and interact with each other. These are the ages the characters should be portrayed, not the ages of the actors portraying them. There had been a tendency to portray many of these characters as much older than they actually are, particularly Dr. Rank but also Nora. Accurately portraying them as the ages described here adds certain dynamics between the characters that makes this show work best. It is not advised to portray the characters as any older than they are listed here.

Ibsen gave no more than a one-word description of the characters in the original text of *A Doll's House*, but to give them additional dimensions, I've included more defined backgrounds in the character description section. Certain features of the characters included in the character descriptions, such as their background, history, psychological underpinnings, and relationships before the play takes place, while specific to this adaptation only, are always informed by things the characters say or do within the play.

Ibsen never described *A Doll's House* as a drama, as he did with some of his other plays. There are many humorous and lighthearted moments in the play. I encourage you to find all the joy and humor that's present throughout the play, which makes its heartbreaking ending all the more powerful.

Reading note: Stage directions are italicized. If this is presented as a staged reading or an audio-only production or podcast, note that stage directions in [brackets] are *not* meant to be read.

Time
The late 1800s, but Ibsen also intended it to be set in the present time.

Place
A port city in Norway, likely Bergen, although Ibsen never specified.

Characters
Everyone in that house is a doll, in one sense or another. Nora is not the only one. Everyone (with the possible exception of Anne-Marie) tries to play everyone else.

Nora Helmer (she/her) 29/30: Nora's very smart and exceedingly bright. She may be naïve, but her naïveté comes from her lack of experience, not lack of intelligence. She grew up fairly well off (she had a private nanny, and maids, after all) which explains her inclination for extravagance. She's only learned one way of getting what she wants out of the male figures in her life, which is to act innocent and helpless, getting them to do what she wants but making them think it's their idea. Nora's an only child with no mother-figure aside from Anne-Marie. She never faced any real consequence in her life, until her dilemma with Nils. In her final conversation with Torvald, she's as much trying to convince herself that she needs to leave as she is trying to convince Torvald. She's making sense of her decision in the moment and grappling with it. When she says she doesn't want to see the kids again, it's likely because if she does go in to see them, she would've changed her mind about leaving. When she tells Torvald the she doesn't love him anymore, it's not a declaration to him as much as it is a realization for herself.

Torvald Helmer (he/him) 34/35: Genuinely believes and shows that he is in love with Nora, and *believes* Nora is in love with him. Likely brought up very religious/conservative, lower middle class or poor. That comes across in how he casually incorporates biblical references and phrases into his everyday speech, his views on marriage and children, and his general attitude about money and debt. Nora and her father were living better than he did with his parents when he was younger. He's worked his way up and he's proud of what he has accomplished and how far he's gotten himself at a relatively young age, but he always fears losing it all and going back to the underprivileged way he grew up. He's very aware that the sophisticated and privileged façade he's put up can crumble with the slightest blunder. That's why he's so afraid of what people think and how people perceive him. That's also why Nils being so informal with Torvald is such a big deal to him but to Nora it seems petty. Perhaps his parents did not have an ideal relationship, and so he's spent his life trying to avoid the mistakes his parents made. His views on the role and duties of a husband, aside from being informed by his religion, may be formed as a reaction to the way his father treated his mother. In his final conversation with Nora, he may be reminded of his parent's relationship, particularly what he viewed as his father's failure as a husband, and therefore he views Nora's betrayal as much her fault as it is his failure to be a proper husband to her. This exacerbates his shame and anger at the situation even more.

Kristine Linde (she/her) 34/35: Kristine is, as she describes herself, very practical. She's very much a realist. It's not so much that fantasies and jokes go over her head, it's just that for so long she just had to be so serious about everything that she's lost a bit of her silly, humorous side. That's why Rank's jokes and Nora's fantasies about a secret admirer go over her head. She and Nora have been childhood friends, so there were parts of their personalities and backgrounds that drew them together at the time. It's likely that Kristine had not been as well off as Nora as kids and so their friendship developed out of convenience for both: Nora needed a girl near her age to talk to and play with, and Kristine may have escaped her lower middle class home to find refuge in playing at Nora's. Nora would tell her stories and they would play with dolls, and for a bit Kristine would feel like she's living a life that she wanted or deserved. When she arrives to visit Nora, she may be hoping to have some of that privileged life back. Maybe she heard that Torvald had some good news coming to him. Maybe she heard through the grapevine that things for the Helmers are changing, and maybe she can rely on her old friend again to help her get back into that privileged life that she felt she had when she and Nora played together as kids. As opposed to Nora, Kristine makes a conscious decision to get back into a relationship. However, unlike Nora, she starts her new relationship on equal footing with her partner. She ends up with the "real marriage" the Nora wished she had with Torvald.

Nils Krogstad (he/him) 34/35: Nils is not an evil, malicious, unscrupulous character, as he is sometimes portrayed. He's a clever, complex, and in many ways a very empathetic character, much more so than Torvald. He and Torvald likely started off on very similar footing socially and financially. Due to various circumstances, not the least of which is how he was burned by Kristine, he started to make some wrong decisions, and as a result, he and Torvald's path in life diverged. He was likely very much affected by his breakup with Kristine to the point where he had resolved to better his circumstances regardless of the means, so as to never end up heartbroken again for lacking status or money. At his core, he needs to be a good character who happened to make some wrong choices and grapples with the mistakes he made, otherwise his sudden change of heart in Act III makes no sense for him. He's not malicious toward, nor does he find any joy at all, in him having to blackmail Nora. He loathes the fact that he even has to do this, and is resentful toward Torvald for putting him in this situation. In fact, the whole ordeal has nothing to do with Nora at all; it's only ever been about Torvald. Just as Torvald has no idea who the real Nora is, he also has no idea who the real Nils is, and anything Torvald says about Nils should not at all be taken as fact. Between Nils and Torvald, Nils is in fact the better person. There are a lot of similarities between his and Kristine's personalities; that's one of the reasons why they work so well together and why their relationship is that of equals. Out of everyone in the play, he and Kristine are the only ones to have a happy ending, and we as the audience have to be genuinely happy for them.

Dr. Rank (he/him) 35-40: Rank is neither gloomy nor miserable, rather he has a dark sense of humor that others who don't know him or who don't understand his sense of humor may interpret as him being depressed or bad tempered. He's very quick witted. He's always been well aware of his condition, and the fact that he will probably die young, and he's handled it by making fun of the situation to himself. He's a very warm character, in his own way, and that's part of the reason Nora's drawn to him. Nora views Rank as a substitute for the things she would like to do with Torvald (have conversations about what she likes, talk about her childhood and friends, have someone to confide in a bit) and things she may have had with her father (an older respected male figure, someone who might be able to answer her questions about life). Nora's relationship with Rank and Torvald is a combination of what she had with her father and what she wants out of a marriage. She's trying to cobble together this singular figure, an ideal husband, out of these two men. As such, Rank has to complement and in some ways overlap with the qualities that Torvald has. That also explains why Torvald and Rank are such close friends. Torvald as Rank says, is a man with a certain sense of fine sensibilities (at least that's how Torvald presents himself), and as such he's very careful with who he chooses to be friends with. He may view Rank as someone to look up to, if not certainly as an equal. Rank is intelligent, and comes from a reputable wealthy family, considering he has inherited a fortune, in contrast to Torvald who likely grew up poor or lower middle class.

Anne-Marie (she/her) 45/46: Out of everyone in the play, Anne-Marie is the only one who has no ulterior motives. She had her daughter when she was around 16, and as a result of her circumstances at the time, gave her up and went to work for Nora's father as her nanny. She's been with Nora ever since and as such she knows Nora inside and out. She's very perceptive. She knows when Nora's lying or hiding something, but doesn't want to call her out. She would do anything to keep Nora from being hurt or uncomfortable, even at her own expense.

Helena (she/her) 20-25: Helena should be portrayed more than just an ordinary maid. Out of everyone, she's the only one who knows everything that's going on. She likely overheard many conversations in the house, including Nora's and Kristine's catch-up chat, Nils blackmailing Nora, and Nora's flirtations with Dr. Rank. She could basically write this play from her recollections of what she witnessed as the Helmer's maid. However, as the maid, she can never really say anything. As such, whenever she appears, she always tries to hide the fact that she knows what's going on, often unsuccessfully, and because others pay little attention to her, they don't notice her reactions or expressions. There's always subtext to what she says. Helena may appear on stage at various times, even when it's not specifically written that she enters or exits. Perhaps you can even see her every now and then appearing to listen in on a conversation.

Ivar, Bob, and Emmy: The Helmer children are depicted but it's not necessary that they be played by actors in this adaptation, leaving room for creativity in how they're portrayed on stage. Ivar is the oldest of the Helmer children. He's likely 6 or 7 years old. Nora and Torvald went on their trip to Italy right after he was born. Bob is the second-oldest and is likely 4 or 5 years old. Emmy is the youngest and is the only girl. She's likely around 2 years old. If you do choose to use child actors to portray these characters, they should not be portrayed much older than those ages, keeping in mind that Nora and Torvald have only been married 8 years.

ACT I

A cozy-looking room is furnished comfortably and tastefully, but not extravagantly: a sofa, armchairs, a table and accents, and a rocking chair. An upright piano sits at the back, copper engravings hang on the walls, a cabinet is full with porcelain and other small objects, and a small book-case is lined with gilded, leather-bound books. The floors are carpeted and a warm fire burns in the fireplace. It's Christmas Eve.

A doorbell rings in the foyer; shortly after, **HELENA***, the maid, enters from the kitchen and opens the front door revealing* **NORA** *who strolls in humming a tune and feeling cheerful. She's wearing a coat and carrying quite a few packages, which she lays on the table. She leaves the front door open behind her, and through it we see a Christmas tree and a basket, which* **HELENA** *takes and follows* **NORA** *inside.*

NORA.
Hide the Christmas tree carefully, Helena. Make sure the children don't see it until it's been decorated tonight. Give the porter a krone, and tell him he can keep the change.

HELENA *leaves.* ***NORA*** *shuts the door to the foyer and laughs to herself as she takes off her coat. She takes a bag of macaroons from her pocket and eats one or two; then tiptoes cautiously to* ***TORVALD****'s office door and listens.*

NORA.
Yup, he's home.

Still humming, she goes to the table and starts going through the packages. Every now and then she takes a bite from a macaroon. ***TORVALD*** *calls out from inside his office.*

TORVALD.
[off.] Is that a goldfinch tweeting out there?

NORA.
[busy opening some of the packages] Yes, it is!

TORVALD.
[off.] Is there a little kitten bouncing around?

NORA.
Yeah.

TORVALD.
[off.] And when did this kitten come home?

NORA.
Just now.

She puts the bag of macaroons back in her pocket and wipes her mouth.

Come here, Torvald, come see what I bought.

TORVALD.
[off.] Not now.

A second later, he opens his door and looks out into the room, pen still in hand.

Did you say "bought"?! *All* these things? Has this little goldfinch been out wasting money again?

NORA.
Yes but, Torvald, this year we really *can* let loose a little. This is the first Christmas where we haven't had to be thrifty.

TORVALD.
That doesn't mean we can start throwing money around.

NORA.
Oh come on, Torvald, we can throw a little money around now, can't we? Just a teeny tiny bit! After all, you're gonna have a large salary and make tons and tons of money.

TORVALD.
Yes, *after* the New Year, and then it'll be a whole quarter before I'm even paid. Three months!

NORA.
Whatever! I'm sure we can borrow until then.

TORVALD.
Nora!

He goes to her and jokingly tweaks her ear.

Being a little frivolous again, are we? Imagine, now, that I borrowed a thousand kroner today, and you spent it all Christmas week, and then on New Year's Eve a brick falls on my head, kills me, and—

Putting her hands over his mouth.

NORA.
Oh, come on! Don't you say ugly things like that!

TORVALD.
Still, imagine that *did* happened,—what then?

NORA.
If something that horrible *did* happen, I don't think it would make much of a difference if I owed any money.

TORVALD.
Ok, but what about the people I borrowed it from?

NORA.
The people you—? Who cares about them? They're strangers.

TORVALD.
[teasingly] Nora, Nora, thou art a woman! No, but seriously, Nora, you know what I think about all this. No debt. Never borrow! A home built on a foundation of borrowing and debt is nothing more than an ugly prison. We held out pretty well so far, and we'll just have to keep doing what we've been doing as long as we need to.

She shuffles to the fireplace.

NORA.
Yeah, yeah, whatever you want, Torvald.

He follows her.

TORVALD.
Now, now, this little goldfinch shouldn't be drooping her wings. What? Is kitten pouting now?

[taking out his wallet] Nora, what do you think I have here?

NORA.
[turning around excitedly] Money!

TORVALD.
There you go.

He hands her some cash.

My God, of course I know how much money you need at Christmas!

NORA.
[counting] Ten, twenty, thirty, forty! Thank you, thank you, Torvald! I'll make sure it'll last me a *long* time!

TORVALD.
Well, it's gonna have to.

NORA.
Yes, yes, it will. But first come here and let me show you everything I got. And all so *cheap*! Some new outfits and a sword for Ivar; a horse and trumpet

for Bob; and a doll with a bed for Emmy—it's pretty plain, but she'll end up breaking it to pieces anyway. And I also got some new dresses and scarves for the maids and Anne-Marie. She really should've had a lot more.

TORVALD.
And what's in this one?

NORA.
[crying out] Torvald, no, no, no! You're not allowed to see that that until tonight!

TORVALD.
All right. But now tell me, you little spendthrift, what do you want for yourself?

NORA.
Oh, gosh…for me? I don't really think I want anything.

TORVALD.
Of course you do! Now tell me something *reasonable* that you want.

NORA.
No, I really can't think of anything—unless, Torvald—

TORVALD.
Yeah?

She plays with his suit buttons without looking at him

NORA.
If you *really* wanna give me something I *want*, you could—I guess—

TORVALD.
Come on, just say it.

NORA.
[speaking quickly] You could give me money! *Only* what you can afford, and then one of these days I'll buy something for myself with it.

TORVALD.
Nora—

NORA.
Oh, yes, please, honey, please, I'm begging you! I'll even wrap it up in some beautiful gold paper and hang it on the Christmas tree. Wouldn't that be fun?

TORVALD.
[feigning ignorance] What're those expensive little birds called that some people enjoy wasting money on?

NORA.
Yes, yes, goldfinches—I know. But just do this for me, Torvald, and then I'll have time to think about what I *really* need. Now doesn't that make more sense? Yes?

TORVALD.
[smiling] Yes it does—that's, of course, assuming you really did save the money I give you, and then really did use it to buy something for yourself. But if instead you end up spending it all on housekeeping and a countless number of useless things, then I'll just end up having to fork over even more money.

NORA.
Now, really, Torvald—

TORVALD.
You can't deny it, Nora.

He puts his arms around her waist.

This little goldfinch is cute, but she sure spends a whole lot of money. It's amazing how expensive it is for a man to keep a goldfinch these days.

NORA.
Oh, come on, how can you even say that to me? I really try to save everything I can.

TORVALD.
[laughing] That's very true—everything you *can*. Trouble is, you can't save anything!

NORA.
[smiling] Well you don't have a clue how many expenses goldfinches and kittens have, Torvald.

TORVALD.
You're a strange little thing, Nora. Just like your father. You always try to get your hands on some money, but as soon as you have it, it just slips through your fingers. You never know where it went. Well, I guess I'll just have to take you as you are. After all, it's in the blood. Yes, yes, it's true, those things *are* inherited.

NORA.
Well, I wish I inherited a lot more of dad's qualities.

TORVALD.
And I wouldn't want you to be any different than exactly how you are, my

sweet little goldfinch. But, you know, it just occurred to me that you're looking a little—how should I say this—a little suspicious today?

NORA.
I do?

TORVALD.
You really do. Here, look at me.

NORA.
[looks at him] Well?

TORVALD.
[wagging his finger at her] Miss Sweet Tooth hasn't been on a rampage through town today, has she?

NORA.
No, why would you even ask that?

TORVALD.
Huh, so Miss Sweet Tooth didn't make a little detour to the bakery?

NORA.
No, I can assure you, Torvald—

TORVALD.
Didn't nibble on some jam?

NORA.
No, definitely not.

TORVALD.
Not even gnawed on a macaroon or two?

NORA.
No, Torvald, now honestly—

TORVALD.
Well, well, well…you know I'm only joking, right?

She coyly moves away from him.

NORA.
It really wouldn't even occur to me to do something you didn't want me to.

TORVALD.
No, I know that. Besides, you did give me your word.

He walks up to her.

Well, keep your little Christmas surprises to yourself, sweetheart. Everything will be revealed this evening by the light of the Christmas tree.

NORA.
Did you remember to invite Doctor Rank?

TORVALD.
No. But there's really no need. Obviously he knows he has an open invitation. But, I can still ask him when he stops by this afternoon. You know, I even ordered some *excellent* wine. Nora, you just can't imagine how much I'm looking forward to this evening.

NORA.
Me too! Not to mention how excited the kids will be, Torvald!

TORVALD.
You know, it really feels amazing to have a perfectly stable job, and a big enough income. It's kind of delightful to think about, isn't it?

NORA.
It's divine!

TORVALD.
Do you remember last Christmas? For three whole weeks, you shut yourself up every night until way past midnight, making ornaments for the Christmas tree, and all kinds of other spectacular things you wanted to surprise us with. It was three of the most boring weeks I've ever spent in my life!

NORA.
I didn't think it was so boring.

TORVALD.
[smiling] But you have to admit, the end result was a little shabby.

NORA.
Oh God, are you gonna tease me about that again? How was I supposed to know that the cat would sneak in and tear everything apart?

TORVALD.
Of course you wouldn't've known, my poor little Nora. You had the best intentions to make us all happy, and that's what matters. But it's definitely a good thing that our hard times are finally over.

NORA.
Yeah, it really is divine.

TORVALD.
This time I don't need to sit here and be bored all alone, and you don't need to ruin those precious eyes and your pretty little hands—

NORA.
[clapping her hands] No, Torvald, I don't need to now, do I? It's so divinely exquisite to hear you say that! Now let me tell you how I've been thinking we should arrange the furniture around here. As soon as Christmas is over—

A bell rings in the foyer.

The doorbell?

She quickly tidies up around the room a little.

Ugh, someone's coming. What a pain!

TORVALD.
If it's a visitor, remember, I'm not at home.

HELENA *comes to the door.*

HELENA.
There's a woman here asking to see you, Mrs. Helmer—a stranger. She didn't give her name.

NORA.
A stranger? Oh, ok well ask her to come in.

HELENA.
[to TORVALD] The doctor's also here to see you, Mr. Helmer. He got here at the same time.

TORVALD.
Did he go straight into my office?

HELENA.
Yes he did.

TORVALD *goes to his office.* **HELENA** *ushers in* **MRS. KRISTINE LINDE**, *who's in her traveling clothes, then goes out and shuts the door.*

KRISTINE.
[nervous and a little hesitant] How are you, Nora?

NORA.
[doubtfully] How are you…

KRISTINE.
I'm guessing you probably don't recognize me.

NORA.
Well, I don't know—yeah, I think I do—*[Suddenly.]* Yeah, of course! Kristine! Is it really you?

KRISTINE.
Yup, it's me.

NORA.
Kristine! I can't believe I almost didn't recognize you! But then how could I—*[In a gentle voice.]* Kristine, you've changed a lot!

KRISTINE.
Yeah, I definitely have. In nine, ten long years—

NORA.
Has it really been that long since we last saw each other? I guess it has. These past eight years have definitely been a happy time for me, let me tell you. But now you're here in town! Did you take a long trip right in the middle of winter?—that's gutsy of you.

KRISTINE.
I got in on the steamer early this morning.

NORA.
To have a little fun during Christmas, of course! Oh, how divine! We'll have so much fun together! But please, please, take off your coat. You're not cold, I hope? Why don't we sit down by the fireplace and be cozy. No, please sit in this armchair. I'll take the rocking chair.

NORA helps KRISTINE with her coat and they sit by the fire. She then takes KRISTINE'S hands in hers, looks closely at her face, and smiles.

Now you look like your old self again. It was just in that first moment—you're a little paler, Kristine, and maybe a bit thinner.

KRISTINE.
And much, much older, Nora.

NORA.
Ok, maybe a *little* older...very, very little...definitely not much. *[Stops suddenly and speaks seriously.]* Ugh, how inconsiderate of me, just sitting here chatting away like this. Kristine, please forgive me.

KRISTINE.
Forgive you for what?

NORA.
[gently] Poor thing, you're a widow now.

KRISTINE.
Yeah, it's been three years.

NORA.
Yes, I heard! I read it in the papers. Please believe me, Kristine, I meant to write you at the time, but I kept putting it off and something always got in the way.

KRISTINE.
I totally understand.

NORA.
No, it was pretty bad on my part. You poor thing, you must've been through so much. And he really left you nothing to live on?

KRISTINE.
No.

NORA.
And no children?

KRISTINE.
Nope.

NORA.
Nothing at all, then.

KRISTINE.
Not even a sense of grief or sorrow to keep me warm at night.

NORA.
[looking incredulously at her] But, Kristine, how's that even possible?

KRISTINE.
[smiles sadly] It sometimes happens, Nora.

NORA.
So you're pretty much alone? That must be awful! I have three exquisite kids. I'd introduce them, but they're out with their nanny. Well, now you have to tell me all about you.

KRISTINE.
No, no, no! I wanna hear about *you*.

NORA.
No, you first. I *can't* be selfish today; today I only wanna think about you and your needs. Well, there is *one* thing I do wanna tell you. Did you hear we just had an incredible bit of good news?

KRISTINE.
No, really?

NORA.
If you can imagine, my husband has been made director of the Commercial Bank!

KRISTINE.
Your husband? That *is* good news!

NORA.
Yes, *incredible*! An attorney's income is so unreliable these days, especially if he's only willing to take on the best of the best; of course those are the only types of clients Torvald's been willing to accept, and I *completely* agree with him. You wouldn't believe just how happy we are! He's starting his work at the Bank right after the New Year, and then he'll have a huge salary and lots of commissions. We can now live very differently than we used to—we can do exactly what we want. Kristine, I just feel so light and happy! It'll be so exquisite to have a ton of money and not have to worry at all anymore, won't it?

KRISTINE.
Well, I guess it would be "exquisite" to have what one needs.

NORA.
No, not just what one *needs*, but so. much. money.

KRISTINE.
[smiling] Nora, Nora, honey, you haven't changed a bit, have you? In our schooldays you were always a little bit extravagant.

NORA.
[laughing] Yeah, that's what Torvald says now. *[Wags her finger at her.]* But "Nora, Nora" isn't as silly as you think. No, we haven't really been in a position for me be extravagant. We've actually *both* had to work.

KRISTINE.
You too?

NORA.
Yeah, you know, just little things: needlework, crocheting, embroidery, that kind of stuff. *[Nonchalantly]* Among other things. Did you know Torvald resigned from his post at the civil service when we got married? There were no prospects for promotion there, and he had to try and earn more than he did before. But during that first year he burned himself out. He had to make money any which way he could, and he would work very early and very late.

But in the end he couldn't handle it and got seriously sick, and the doctors told me that he should take a sabbatical down south.

KRISTINE.
Yeah, you spent a whole year in Italy, didn't you?

NORA.
We did. And it wasn't exactly easy to get away, I can tell you that much. It was right after Ivar was born. But of course we *had* to go. It was such a divinely exquisite trip, and it saved Torvald's life. But it cost a fortune, Kristine.

KRISTINE.
I can imagine.

NORA.
Four thousand eight hundred kroner. That's a whole lot of money, isn't it?

KRISTINE.
Yeah, and in emergencies like that it's fortunate to have that money.

NORA.
Yeah, well, if you wanna know, we got it from my dad, of course.

KRISTINE.
Oh, I see. That was right around the time he died, wasn't it?

NORA.
It was. And I couldn't even go and be there with him, nurse him back to health. I was expecting Ivar's birth any minute and I had my poor, sick Torvald to take care of. My precious father—I never saw him again, Kristine. That was the hardest thing I've experienced in my whole marriage.

KRISTINE.
I knew you were very fond of him…So then you went off to Italy?

NORA.
Yeah, well, we had the money then, and the doctors insisted that we go, so we left a month later.

KRISTINE.
And your husband came back completely cured?

NORA.
Right as rain!

KRISTINE.
But then—the doctor?

NORA.
What doctor?

KRISTINE.
I thought the man who got here at the same time as me was a doctor?

NORA.
Oh, yeah, that's Doctor Rank, but he doesn't come here on house calls. He's our closest friend, and drops by at least once a day. No, Torvald hasn't been sick at all since then, and our kids are strong and healthy, and so am I.

NORA jumps up and claps her hands in content.

Oh, God, Kristine! It is divinely exquisite to be alive and happy!—Ugh, but it's so gross of me to just be talking about myself and my problems again.

*She sits on a nearby ottoman and rests her hands **KRISTINE'S** knees.*

Please don't be annoyed with me. Tell me, is it really true that you didn't love your husband? Why did you even marry him?

KRISTINE.
He asked. My mother was alive at the time, but she was sick and helpless. I also had two younger brothers to take care of, so it didn't seem responsible on my part to reject his offer.

NORA.
No, you probably did the right thing. Was he rich?

KRISTINE.
I think he was fairly well off. But his business was unreliable, and, when he died, it all fell apart and there was nothing left.

NORA.
And then?—

KRISTINE.
Then I had to move on and take any job I could find—a small shop at first, then a small school, and so on. The last three years have felt like a very long workday, with no rest. But it's all over, Nora. My mom doesn't need me anymore, now that she passed away. And the boys don't need me either; they're all grown and can take care of themselves.

NORA.
Wow, you must feel pretty relieved now that—

KRISTINE.
No, Nora. I only feel that my life is indescribably empty. No one to live for, anymore.

She stands up in her restlessness.

That's why I couldn't stand the life I had in that little town anymore. I'm hoping it might be easier here to find something that'll keep me busy and occupy my thoughts. If only I could have the good fortune to get some regular work—office work of some kind—

NORA.
But, Kristine, that's so strenuous, and you already look exhausted. You're much better off going away to a spa.

KRISTINE.
I don't have a father to give me money for a trip, Nora.

NORA.
Oh, don't be angry with me!

KRISTINE.
It's you who shouldn't be angry with me. The worst thing about being in my situation is that it floods your mind with so much bitterness. You have no one to work for, but still you somehow find yourself constantly busy and always on edge waiting for an opportunity to strike. You have to live, and so you become selfish. When you shared your good news—would you believe it?—I was thrilled, not so much for you, but for myself.

NORA.
What do you mean?—Oh, I see. You mean that maybe Torvald might be able to help you out?

KRISTINE.
Yes, that's exactly what I meant.

NORA.
Well so he will, Kristine. Just leave it to me; I'll be very *subtle* about it—I'll have to come up with something that'll put him in a very good mood. Oh, Kristine, I really, *really* wanna be able to help you!

KRISTINE.
It's very nice of you to be so excited about helping me. Particularly nice for someone who knows so little about the troubles and hardships of this life.

NORA.
I know so little about—?

KRISTINE.
[smiling] Well, my God! Ok, sure, small household chores and that type of thing!—you're practically a kid, Nora.

NORA shakes her head and walks away from her.

NORA.
You don't have to be so condescending about it.

KRISTINE.
Condescending?

NORA.
You're just like the others. They all think I'm no good at doing *anything* serious—

KRISTINE.
Come on, now—

NORA.
—that I haven't accomplished anything in this world.

KRISTINE.
Nora, honey, you *just* told me all about your troubles.

NORA.
Whatever!—that was only a taste.

*She walks to **KRISTINE** and whispers.*

I haven't told you about the *big one.*

KRISTINE.
The big one? What do you mean?

NORA.
You underestimate me, Kristine—but you shouldn't. You're probably proud that you worked so hard and so long for your mother.

KRISTINE.
I certainly don't underestimate anybody. But it's true: I'm both proud and happy to have had the privilege of keeping my mother comfortable in her final years.

NORA.
And you're also proud of what you've done for your brothers?

KRISTINE.
I think I earned the right to be.

NORA.
I think so, too. Well then, how about this; I also have something that makes me proud and happy.

KRISTINE.
I don't doubt that. But what exactly do mean?

NORA.
Come here, I don't want Torvald to hear! He can't know, no matter what—no one in the world can know, Kristine, except for you.

KRISTINE.
Well, what is it?

NORA.
Come here.

*She sits on the sofa and pulls **KRISTINE** down next to her.*

I saved Torvald's life.

KRISTINE.
"Saved"? What do you mean "saved"?

NORA.
I already told you about our sabbatical in Italy. The truth is Torvald would've died if he hadn't gone there—

KRISTINE.
Yeah, but your father gave you the money for that.

NORA.
[smiling] Yes, that's what Torvald and everyone else think, but—

KRISTINE.
But—

NORA.
Dad didn't give us anything. *I* got the money.

KRISTINE.
You? The whole amount?

NORA.
Four thousand eight hundred kroner. What do you think about that?

KRISTINE.
Yeah, but, Nora, how's that possible? Did you win the Lottery?

NORA.
[contemptuously] The Lottery? What talent would that have taken?

KRISTINE.
Well where'd you get it from, then?

NORA hums and smiles mysteriously.

Because you couldn't have borrowed it.

NORA.
Couldn't I? Why not?

KRISTINE.
No, a wife can't borrow without her husband's consent.

NORA.
But, if it's a wife who *happens* to be a bit business savvy—a wife who knows how to be a bit—shrewd—

KRISTINE.
Ok, Nora, I'm not following you at all.

NORA.
Well, you don't need to! I never said I *borrowed* the money. Maybe I got it some other way. Maybe I got it from a secret admirer. When you're as attractive as I am—

KRISTINE.
You're crazy.

NORA.
Piqued your interest, have I, Kristine?

KRISTINE.
You haven't been reckless, have you?

NORA.
Is it reckless to save your husband's life?

KRISTINE.
I think it would be reckless if, without his knowledge, you—

NORA.
But he just *couldn't* know anything! Oh my God, how can you not get that? He couldn't even know how bad his health had gotten. The doctors came to *me* and told *me* that his life was in danger, and that the only thing that would save him was a long sabbatical down south. Do you think I didn't try, first of all, to get him to do it by making him think that it was all for me?

I told him how *exquisite* it would be for me to travel abroad like all the other young wives. I cried and I begged. I told him he should consider the situation I was in, and that he should be kind and generous to me. I even hinted that he could take out a loan. That practically made him livid. He called me frivolous, and said it was his duty as a husband not to indulge my whims and fantasies—his exact words, I believe. Well then, I thought, someone *needs* to save him—and so I figured out a way—

KRISTINE.
And your husband didn't learn from your dad that the money didn't really come from him?

NORA.
Nope, never. Dad died around that same time. I really thought about telling him about it and begging him not to tell anyone. But by that point he'd gotten so sick and—unfortunately, that never became necessary.

KRISTINE.
And you've never trusted your husband with your secret since?

NORA.
Oh God, no! How painful and humiliating would it be for Torvald, with his masculine pride, to know that he owed *me* anything? It would disrupt the entire balance of our relationship; our beautiful, happy home wouldn't be what it is.

KRISTINE.
So you'll never tell him?

NORA.
[meditatively, and with a half smile] Maybe—someday, after a long time, when I'm not as pretty as I am now. Don't laugh! I mean, you know, when Torvald doesn't adore me as much as he does now. When he doesn't take pleasure anymore in having me dance and act and dress-up in costumes for him; that's when it might be good to have something like that in my pocket— *[Breaking off.]* Heh, listen to me babble on! That time is never gonna come.

So, what do you think of my big secret, Kristine? Would you now agree that I'm also good for something? And by the way, you wouldn't *believe* how much anxiety this whole thing has given me. It definitely hasn't been easy for me to keep up with all the obligations that came with this loan.

Let me tell you, in the business world there are things called "quarterly interest" and "installments," and it's not exactly the easiest thing to manage them. I've had to save a little here and there, whatever I could. I couldn't really skim much off the household budget, since Torvald expects to live well. And I'm definitely not gonna let my kids walk around all poorly dressed, either, so I've also had to spend every last bit of the money he gives me for their expenses, the sweet little things!

KRISTINE.
So it all had to come out of your own allowance?

NORA.
Yeah, of course. But then again I was also in the best position to do that without anyone suspecting anything. Whenever Torvald gave me money for new dresses and things like that, I never spent more than half of it. I'd always buy the simplest and cheapest things. Thank God that basically *anything* looks good on me; that's only reason Torvald's never really noticed. But it's been very hard on me, Kristine because—well, it's just so exquisite to be *really* well dressed, you know what I mean?

KRISTINE.
Oh, yeah, sure.

NORA.
I also found other ways of making money. Last winter I was lucky enough to get a lot of copying work. So I locked myself up and sat writing every night until way past midnight. And I'd get so tired. *So* tired, Kristine! Still, it was kind of fun to sit there working and earning money. I felt almost like a man.

KRISTINE.
And how much have you been able to pay off that way?

NORA.
I can't say exactly. It's pretty hard keeping track of these kinds of things, you know? I can only say that I paid every last bit that I could scrape together. I got fed up so many times. *[Smiles.]* Sometimes I'd sit here and think about a rich old man who fell in love with me—that he died, and then when his will was read, it said, in big letters: "All my money shall be paid immediately and in cash to the gracious Mrs. Nora Helmer."

KRISTINE.
But, Nora, honey—who would that be?

NORA.
Oh my God, do you not get it? That's just a fantasy I made up in my head over and over, when I couldn't think of any other way of making money. But with Torvald's new job, none of that matters now. I can just sit and be carefree.

God, that's so exquisite to think about, Kristine! Carefree! To be free from care; to be able to play with the kids and keep a beautiful home and have everything just the way Torvald likes it! And, just think, spring is right around the corner with that big blue sky! Maybe we'll take a little trip—see the sea again! Oh, it really is divine to be alive and happy.

A bell rings in the foyer.

KRISTINE.
There's the doorbell. I probably should get going.

NORA.
No, please stay! No one's coming in here. It's probably for Torvald.

HELENA opens the door to the foyer and looks in.

HELENA.
Excuse me, Mrs. Helmer—there's a man here asking to talk to the attorney—

NORA.
To the *Bank Director*, you mean?

HELENA.
…Yes, to the Bank Director…But I wasn't sure, since the doctor's there with him—

NORA.
And who is it?

NILS KROGSTAD pops up from behind HELENA and stands at the door.

NILS
It's me, Mrs. Helmer.

KRISTINE flinches, trembles, and turns awkwardly to the window. Nora takes a step towards NILS.

NORA.
[*speaking in a strained, low voice*] You? What is it? What do you want to talk to my husband about?

NILS.
Bank business—if you will. I do some work at the Commercial Bank, and I heard your husband's going to be our new boss—

NORA.
Then it's—

NILS.
Just some boring business. Absolutely nothing else.

NORA.
Would you mind going to his office through the foyer, then.

She waves him off indifferently, shuts the door, and then goes to stoke the fire in the fireplace.

KRISTINE.
Nora—who was that man?

NORA.
A lawyer. His name is Nils Krogstad.

KRISTINE.
So that really was him.

NORA.
You know him?

KRISTINE.
I used to—several years ago. He used to be a solicitor's clerk in our town.

NORA.
Yes, he was.

KRISTINE.
He changed a lot.

NORA.
I think he was in a very unhappy marriage.

KRISTINE.
He's a widower now, isn't he?

NORA.
With a few children. There, now, nice and warm.

KRISTINE.
They say he does all kinds of work now.

NORA.
Oh yeah? Maybe he does. I wouldn't know anything about it. But let's not talk about work; it's so boring!

DOCTOR RANK comes out of TORVALD'S office, speaking to the unseen TORVALD before he closes the door.

RANK.
No, no, my friend, I don't want to intrude; I'd rather visit your wife for a bit.

He shuts the door and then notices KRISTINE.

Excuse me, I'm afraid I'm intruding here too.

NORA.
No, not at all. *[Introducing him]* Doctor Rank, Kristine Linde.

RANK.
Oh, yes, I've heard your name mentioned here fairly often. I think I went past you on the stairs.

KRISTINE.
Yes, I walked up here a little too slow. I can't handle stairs very well.

RANK.
Ahh! Organs getting a little rotten already?

KRISTINE.
Actually, it's more the fact that I've been overworking myself.

RANK.
Nothing else? Then I assume you've come to town to join in on all the Christmas cheer?

KRISTINE.
I came to look for work.

RANK.
Is that the standard treatment for overwork?

KRISTINE.
You have to live, Doctor Rank.

RANK.
Yes, that seems to be the general consensus these days.

NORA.
Oh, now, Doctor Rank—you know you wanna live.

RANK.
Yes, I really do. However miserable I might feel, I'd like the agony to last as long as possible. All my medical patients feel the same way. As do those who are *morally* diseased; one of them, who has a bad case of it by the way, is with Torvald right now—

KRISTINE sighs sadly.

NORA.
Who're you talking about?

RANK.
A lawyer named Nils Krogstad, a guy you don't know at all. Rotten to the core, Nora! He also started talking about how much he wants to live.

NORA.
Did he now? What did he wanna talk to Torvald about?

RANK.
Not a clue; I only heard that it was something to do with the Commercial Bank.

NORA.
I didn't know that Nil—that this lawyer—Krogstad had anything to do with the Commercial Bank.

RANK.
Yeah, he has a minor job over there. *[To **KRISTINE**.]* I don't know if, where you're from, you have the sort of people who go sniffing around enthusiastically, trying to catch a whiff of moral decay, and, as soon as they've found the source, put that sick person into some lucrative position for the sole purpose of keeping an eye on him. The healthy ones end up left out in the cold.

KRISTINE.
Well, it's the sick who have more of a need to be brought in and taken care of.

RANK.
[shrugging his shoulders] And there you have it. That's the mentality that's turning society into an insane asylum.

NORA, who had been absorbed in her thoughts, breaks out into stifled giggling and claps her hands.

RANK.
Why're you laughing about that? Do you have any idea what society is really about?

NORA.
Why would I care about boring society? I'm laughing at something else, something really funny. Tell me, Doctor Rank, are all the employees at the Commercial Bank dependent on Torvald now?

RANK.
Is *that* what you find really funny?

NORA.
[smiling and humming] Never mind, never mind!

She walks aimlessly around the room.

Although, it really *is* funny that we have—that Torvald has so much power over so many people now.

She takes the bag of macaroons from her pocket.

Doctor Rank, would you care for a little macaroon?

RANK.
A macaroon? I thought they were banned around here.

NORA.
Yes, but Kristine gave me these.

KRISTINE.
What? I did—?

NORA.
Now, now, don't worry! There's no way you would've known that Torvald had banned them. If you wanna know, he's just afraid they'll rot my beautiful teeth. But, hey—one couldn't hurt—isn't that right, Doctor Rank? Here you go!

*She pops a macaroon into **RANK'S** mouth.*

You too, Kristine. And while we're at it, I guess I'll have one myself; just a tiny one—ok, maybe two.

*She gives **KRISTINE** a macaroon and takes one or two for herself while continuing to walk aimlessly around the room.*

Ok, now I *really* feel happy. There's only one thing left in the world that I'd absolutely love to do.

RANK.
Oh? Well, what is it?

NORA.
I have this incredible urge to say something in front of Torvald.

RANK.
And why can't you say it?

NORA.
No, I really can't, it's so gross.

KRISTINE.
Gross?

RANK.
Well, then, I wouldn't advise you to say it. But, maybe you can tell *us*. What do you have an incredible urge to say in front of Torvald?

NORA.
I have an incredible urge to say:—damn it all to hell!

RANK.
Are you insane?

KRISTINE.
Oh, God, Nora…

RANK.
Well, here's your chance, sounds like he's coming!

She hides the bag back in her pocket and hastily gestures to them to be quiet. **TORVALD** *comes out of his office, with his coat over his arm and a hat in his hand.*

NORA.
So, Torvald, honey, did you get rid of him?

TORVALD.
Yeah, he just left.

NORA.
Let me introduce you, then—this is Kristine. She just got into town.

TORVALD.
Kristine—? Sorry, but I don't know—

NORA.
Linde, honey, Kristine Linde.

TORVALD.
Oh, of course. A childhood friend of my wife's, I assume?

KRISTINE.
Yes, we've known each other since then.

NORA.
And imagine, she took a long trip *just* to see you.

TORVALD.
What do you mean?

KRISTINE.
Well, not really—

NORA.
Kristine is *extremely* good at office work, and she's very anxious to work under the guidance of a capable man and learn even more than she already—

TORVALD.
Very practical, Kristine.

NORA.
And when she heard you're now the new director of the Commercial Bank—through a telegram, yes?—she came here quick as she could and—. Torvald, I'm sure you'll be able to do something for her, won't you? For *me*?

TORVALD.
I mean, it's not entirely out of the question. I assume you're windowed, Kristine?

KRISTINE.
Yes.

TORVALD.
And you have experience doing office work?

KRISTINE.
Yeah, plenty.

TORVALD.
Well, then, it's very likely I can find a job for you—

NORA.
[clapping her hands] See? See?

TORVALD.
You actually arrived at a very opportune moment, Kristine.

KRISTINE.
Wow, how can I thank you?

TORVALD.
There's no need. But for now, you'll have to excuse me—

RANK.
Just a minute! I'll come with you.

*As **TORVALD** puts on his coat, **RANK** takes his from the foyer and warms it by the fireplace.*

NORA.
Don't be too long, darling.

TORVALD.
One hour, no more than that.

NORA.
Are you leaving too, Kristine?

***KRISTINE** puts on her coat with **NORA** helping her.*

KRISTINE.
Yes, I have to go and look for a room.

TORVALD.
Oh, well then maybe we can walk down the street together.

NORA.
What a shame that we're so tight on space here; I'm afraid it's impossible for us—

KRISTINE.
Please, don't worry about it! Bye, Nora, and thank you for everything!

NORA.
Bye for now. Of course you're welcome to join us this evening! In fact, I insist. And you too, Dr. Rank. What do you say? If you're feeling well enough? Just make sure to bundle up!

They all walk toward to the front door while chatting with each other. Children's voices are heard coming from the stairwell.

There they are! There they are!

She runs to open the door. **ANNE-MARIE***, the nanny, stands there with the kids and* **NORA** *bends down to kiss them.*

Come in, come in! Oh, you sweet little angels! Look at them, Kristine! Aren't they just divine?

RANK.
Let's not all just stand here in the draft.

TORVALD.
Come on, Kristine. Only a mother can tolerate this place now!

RANK*,* **TORVALD***, and* **KRISTINE** *go downstairs as* **ANNE-MARIE** *comes in with the kids.* **NORA** *closes the door to the foyer and goes to them. The kids talk to her simultaneously as she listens and replies.*

NORA.
You look so handsome! Look at those cheeks, red like apples and roses. Did you have a lot of fun? That's awesome! Yeah? You pulled Emmy *and* Bob on the sled? —at the same time?—that's great! You're a very strong boy, Ivar. *[To* **ANNE-MARIE***]* Here, I'll take her for a little bit, Anne-Marie. My sweet little baby doll!

She takes Emmy, the youngest of the three, from **ANNE-MARIE** *and dances with her.*

Yes, yes, momma will dance with Bob too. What! You made snowballs? I wish I'd been there, too! *[To **ANNE-MARIE**]* No, no, I'll change their outfits myself, Anne-Marie; please let me do it, it's so much fun. You can go warm up in the nursery. You look like you're freezing. There's some hot coffee on the stove for you.

***ANNE-MARIE** goes into the nursery. **NORA** takes off the children's coats and hats and throws them wherever they may land as they all continue to talk to her simultaneously.*

NORA.
Is that so? A big dog came after you? But he didn't bite, did he? No, dogs don't bite nice little baby dolls. No, don't look at the packages, Ivar. What are they? Well wouldn't you like to know? No, no—it's, something—something scary! Come here, let's play a game! What should we play, huh? Hide and Seek? Ok, let's play Hide and Seek. Bob can hide first. Oh, I have to hide first? Ok, I'll hide first.

*She and the children laugh and play in and out of the room. She hides under the table and the children rush in looking for her, but can't seem to find her. They hear her stifled laughter, run to the table, and lift up the cover to find her there. They all scream for joy. She crawls out, as if trying to scare them, resulting in more screams of joy. Meanwhile there had been a knock at the front door, but none of them noticed. The door to the foyer opens halfway, revealing **NILS** who waits a little; the game continues.*

NILS.
Excuse me.

With a stifled cry, she turns around and sits up on to her knees.

NORA.
Oh, you. What do you want?

NILS.
Sorry, the front door was open. Someone must've forgot to close it.

She stands up.

NORA.
My husband's not here, Nils.

NILS.
I know.

NORA.
Why are you here, then?

NILS.
To talk to you.

NORA.
To me?—*[To the children, gently.]* Wanna go find Anne-Marie? What? No, the strange man is not gonna hurt me. When he leaves, we'll play another game, ok?

She takes the children into the nursery and shuts the door after them.

[nervous and tense] So, you want to talk to me?

NILS.
Yes, I do.

NORA.
Today? It's not the first of the month.

NILS.
No, it's Christmas Eve, and it'll be up to you just how merry your Christmas will be.

NORA.
What do you want? Today, I really can't—

NILS.
Oh, we're not gonna talk about *that* just yet. This is about something else. Got a minute?

NORA.
Ok—yes, I do—but—

NILS.
Good. I was just sitting inside Olsen's Restaurant and saw your husband walking down the street—

NORA.
Yes?

NILS.
With a woman.

NORA.
And?

NILS.
May I be so bold to ask, was it Kristine Linde?

NORA.
It was.

NILS.
She's an old friend of yours, isn't she?

NORA.
She is. But I don't see—

NILS.
I knew her, too. Back in the day.

NORA.
Yes, I'm aware.

NILS.
Are you now? So then you know all about it. I thought so. Then can I ask you, without beating about the bush—will Kristine be working at the Bank?

NORA.
Just what exactly gives you the right to interrogate me like this, Nils?—you're nothing more than one of my husband's employees! But, ask and you shall receive, right? Yes, Kristine will have a job at the Bank. And I helped her get it, Nils, I can tell you that much.

NILS.
Just as I thought.

NORA paces around the room.

NORA.
You know, sometimes a person might have a little bit of influence. And just because that person happens to be a woman, it doesn't mean that—. When someone's just a subordinate, Nils, he should be really careful not to offend anyone who—how do I say this—

NILS.
—has a little bit of influence?

NORA.
Exactly.

NILS.
[changing his tone] Nora, would you be kind enough to use your little bit of influence on my behalf.

NORA.
What? What do you mean?

NILS.
It would be so nice of you to make sure that I'm still able to keep my job—as a subordinate—at the Bank.

NORA.
I don't know what you mean. Who wants to take your job away from you?

NILS.
Oh, come on now, there's no need to play dumb with me. Look, I definitely know why your friend's not very keen on the idea of running into me. And now, because of you, I also know who I can thank for being thrown out of a job.

NORA.
I can promise you—

NILS.
Yes, yes, yes; long story short, now's the right time for you to use your "little bit of influence."

NORA.
But, Nils, I don't *have* any influence.

NILS.
You don't? I thought you just said—

NORA.
Look, that's not what I meant. Seriously, now! Why would you think that *I* have that kind of power over my husband?

NILS.
Oh, I've known your husband since our college days. I don't think Mr. Bank Director is any less pliable than other men.

NORA.
If you disrespect my husband again, I swear I'll throw you out that door.

NILS.
M'lady sure is brave.

NORA.
I'm not afraid of you anymore. As soon as the New Year's here, I'll be free of this whole mess before you know it.

NILS.
[controlling himself] Let me be very clear, Nora. If necessary, I'm prepared to fight for this job like I would for my life.

NORA.
Sure seems that way.

NILS.
And it's not even about the money. That's actually what I care about the

least. There's another reason—and I guess I might as well tell you. I assume you know, like everyone else, that, several years ago, I was charged with, shall we say, an indiscretion.

NORA.
I may have heard something about that.

NILS.
It never went to court, but still every door and window were closed to me after that. So I started doing—well, *you* know. I had to do *something*, and, honestly, I don't even think I'm one of the worst. But now I need to break free from all that. My sons are growing up, and for their sake I have to try and win back as much respect as I can in this town. This job at the Bank was like a brand new start for me, a first step—but now your husband wants to kick me down the stairs and back into the dirt.

NORA.
But you have to believe me, Nils! It's not at all in my power to help you.

NILS.
When there's a will, there's a way, Nora. You just don't have the will. But I have ways of changing that.

NORA.
So, what? You're gonna tell my husband that I owe you money?

NILS.
Hmm!—suppose I told him?

NORA.
It would sure be pretty shameful of you. *[Holding back tears.]* To think that he would learn about my secret, a source of joy and pride for me, in this hideous, clumsy way—or that that he would learn about it from *you*! It would put me in an uncomfortable position.

NILS.
Just uncomfortable?

NORA.
[impetuously] Fine, do it, then!—It's not like you'll be any better off. My husband can see for himself what a pathetic excuse for a man you are. Forget about keeping your job, then.

NILS.
What I meant was, you're only worried about being uncomfortable *at home*?

NORA.

If my husband does find out, you *know* he'll pay you everything I still owe, and then you'll be out of our lives completely.

He takes a step towards her.

NILS.

Look, Nora. Either your memory is a little foggy, or you clearly have no idea how this whole business works. So why don't I shed a little light on your situation.

NORA.

What do you mean?

NILS.

When your husband was sick, you came to me to borrow four thousand eight hundred kroner—

NORA.

I didn't know where else to go.

NILS.

And I promised to get you that amount—

NORA.

You sure did.

NILS.

—I promised to get you that amount, with certain conditions. Seems to me that you were so focused on your husband's health, and so anxious to get the money, that you may not have paid enough attention to said conditions. So why don't I remind you? If you remember, I told you that, to get you the money, I would need to draw up a loan agreement, a bond—

NORA.

Which I signed.

NILS.

—yes, but below your signature there were a few lines having to do with naming your father as a co-signer for the loan. Those lines your father was supposed to have signed.

NORA.

Supposed to have? He did sign them.

NILS.

I had left the date line blank. That's to say, your father should've written the date there himself when he signed the bond. You do remember that, don't you?

NORA.
Yes, I believe so—

NILS.
Then I gave it to you to send to your father by mail, yes?

NORA.
Yes.

NILS.
And obviously you did so pretty quickly, because barely five or six days after that, you brought it back to me with your father's signature. And then I gave you the money.

NORA.
Which I've been paying off on time.

NILS.
You have been, yes. But—to stay on topic—that must've been a very difficult time for you, Nora, no?

NORA.
It was.

NILS.
Your father was very sick, wasn't he?

NORA.
He was dying.

NILS.
And he died not long after that?

NORA.
Yes.

NILS.
Tell me, Nora, would you by any chance remember the *exact* date that your father died?

NORA.
September 29th.

NILS.
That's right; I personally verified it. And, so, you see, that's why we seem to have a little discrepancy that I'm just not able to sort out.

He takes out a piece of paper from his pocket and holds it out for **NORA** *to see.*

NORA.
Little discrepancy? I don't know—

NILS.
Your father died on September 29th, but, see here? He dated his signature October 2nd. And doesn't that just seem so strange, Nora?

She's tensely quiet.

Can you maybe help clear that up for me?

She remains quiet.

It's also very interesting that the words "October 2nd," as well as the year, don't seem to be written in your *father's* handwriting, but in one that I think I can recognize. I mean, I guess it's possible that your father forgot to date his signature, and someone else may have filled it in willy-nilly before they knew that he had died. There's really nothing wrong with that. It's the signature that actually matters, and whether it's genuine or not. Isn't that true, Nora?

No answer.

Was it really your father who signed this?

NORA *thinks for a moment, then throws her head up defiantly and glares at him*

NORA.
No, it wasn't. I signed his name.

NILS.
How about that. And you're aware how dangerous a confession like that is?

NORA.
How so? You'll have the rest of your money soon.

NILS.
Let me ask you a question; why didn't you just send the documents to your father?

NORA.
It wasn't possible. He was already very sick, and if I had asked him to sign it, I would've also had to tell him what the money was for. Given his health, I just couldn't bring myself to tell him that my husband's life was in danger—it just wasn't possible.

NILS.
Then it would've been better for you to have given up on the whole thing.

NORA.
No, out of the question. That was to save my husband's life. I couldn't give up on that

NILS.
So it never occurred to you that you were committing fraud against me?

NORA.
You weren't a part of my calculation. I barely even thought about you at all. I couldn't stand you or the heartless way you kept throwing obstacles my way, even though you knew that my husband's life was in danger.

NILS.
You obviously don't realize what kind of predicament you've gotten yourself into. But I can at least tell you that my "indiscretion," the thing that cost me my entire reputation, wasn't any better or worse than what you've done here yourself.

NORA.
You? You actually expect me to believe that you were bold enough to risk your own reputation just to save your wife's life?

NILS.
The law doesn't care about motives.

NORA.
Then it must be a pretty bad law.

NILS.
Bad or not, it's the law you'd have to answer to if I present this evidence in court.

NORA.
This is unbelievable. You're telling me that a daughter is not allowed to spare her dying father from grief and anxiety? That a wife is not allowed to save her husband's life? I may not know much about the law, Nils, but I'm sure that somewhere in there these kinds of things are perfectly legal. You're not even aware of that, are you—and you claim to be a lawyer? Well, then you must be a pretty terrible one at that.

NILS.
Maybe so. But at least when it comes to business—the kind you and I have together—you can bet I understand every last bit of it. Oh well. Do whatever

you want. But let me tell you this—if I'm thrown out on the street a second time, I'll be looking for you to keep me company.

He turns and exits through the foyer. **NORA** *stands silently, buried in her thoughts. After a short while, she looks up and shakes her head.*

NORA.
No, no. He's just trying to scare me!—Like I'm *that* naïve.

She begins to pick up the kids' jackets and hats that she had thrown randomly on the floor.

But—? No, it's impossible! I did it all out of love.

The kids enter timidly from the nursery and ask whether the stranger had left yet. They want to play again. She talks to them as if nothing had happened since they left.

Yes, darlings, he just left. But, let's not tell anyone about the stranger. Ok? Not even daddy. No, no, sweetheart—I can't play now. I know, I promised, but I can't right now. I have so much work to do! Come on, my sweet little angels!

She nudges them gently back into the nursery, shuts the door, and goes to the sofa where she picks her embroidery and sits down absentmindedly sewing a few stitches. After a bit she stops and puts it down, gets up, goes to the door to the foyer, and calls out.

Helena! Bring the Christmas tree in.

She goes to the table and opens a box containing decorations, but stops again.

No, no! It's just not possible!

HELENA *enters with the tree.*

HELENA.
Where should I put it, Mrs. Helmer?

NORA.
Right over there.

Busy with her thoughts, **NORA** *points to the middle of the room without looking and* **HELENA** *sets the tree there.*

HELENA.
Should I get anything else for you?

NORA.
No, thank you, Helena. I have everything I need.

HELENA leaves and NORA walks over to the tree and begins to decorate it.

A candle here, and a flower there—That disgusting man! Nope, nope, nope—there's nothing wrong. The tree will be *exquisite*! I'll do whatever you want, Torvald!—I'll sing for you, dance for you—

TORVALD comes in from the foyer with some documents under his arm.

Oh! You're back already?

TORVALD.
Yes. Was someone just here?

NORA.
Here? No.

TORVALD.
That's odd. I just saw Nils going out the front.

NORA.
Did you? Oh yes, I forgot, he was here for a bit.

TORVALD.
Nora, I can see it in your eyes. Let me guess, he was just here begging you to put in a good word for him.

NORA.
Yes.

TORVALD.
And not only were you supposed to make it look like you were doing it voluntarily, but also to hide the fact that he was even here. Did he ask you to do that, too?

NORA.
Yes, Torvald, but—

TORVALD.
Nora, Nora, how can you even *think* of doing something like this? To have a conversation with him, promise that you'd do something for him, and on top of that lie to me about it!

NORA.
Lie—?

TORVALD.
You just told me to my face that no one was here. *[Wags his finger at her while smiling.]* My little goldfinch should never do that again. A good goldfinch only sings flawlessly, never a false note.

He puts his arms around her waist.

Don't you agree? Yes, that's what I thought. Now, why don't we forget all about it?

He lets her go, walks over to the fireplace and sits down to look through his documents. **NORA** *goes back to decorating the Christmas tree.*

It's so warm and cozy in here!

NORA.
[after a short pause] Torvald!

TORVALD.
Yeah?

NORA.
I'm really looking forward to the masquerade party at the Stenborg's the day after tomorrow.

TORVALD.
And I'm really curious to see what costume you'll be surprising me with.

NORA.
Ugh, *that* stupid thing!

TORVALD.
What do you mean?

NORA.
I just can't think of anything that's good enough. Everything I come up with seems so trivial, so meaningless.

TORVALD.
So my little Nora has finally come to that realization?

She playfully walks over to **TORVALD** *and stands behind him, putting her hands on the back of his chair and peeking over his shoulder. He doesn't pay her much attention.*

NORA.
Are you particularly busy, Torvald?

TORVALD.
Well—

NORA.
What're all those papers for?

TORVALD.
Bank business.

NORA.
Already?

TORVALD.
I just got authority from the retiring Director to make some necessary changes to the staffing and business plan. I need to spend Christmas week working on that if I want everything to be all set in time for the New Year.

NORA.
[quietly to herself] So that's why Nils is—

TORVALD.
Hmm?

She leans against the back of his chair and plays with his hair.

NORA.
If only you weren't so busy, I would've asked you for a huge favor, Torvald.

TORVALD.
What huge favor? Come on now, you can tell me.

NORA.
It's just that—*no one* has a more sophisticated taste than you. And I *really* wanna look stunning at the masquerade party. Torvald, if only you could hold my hand and walk me through all the possible options—

TORVALD.
Ah! So, little Miss Independent's finally admitting she needs a man's help?

NORA.
Yes, Torvald, I really can't get anything done without your help.

TORVALD.
Ok, ok, I'll think about it. I'm sure we can figure something out.

NORA.
That is so incredibly nice of you!

She goes back to decorating the Christmas tree. A short pause.

These red flowers sure look gorgeous, don't they! —So—out of curiosity, what exactly was so awful that this Nils Krogstad guy supposedly did?

TORVALD.
He forged signatures. You know what that means?

NORA.
…Maybe he did it out of a genuine necessity?

TORVALD.
That, or—like so many others—out of recklessness. I'm not so heartless that I would write someone off permanently just because of one bad decision, you know.

NORA.
No, you wouldn't, Torvald.

TORVALD.
Plenty of guilty folks have been able to redeem themselves, provided they confess their crime and accept their punishment.

NORA.
Punishment—?

TORVALD.
But that's not the path Nils chose. He got himself out of it through dishonesty and deceit, and that's why he's now morally bankrupt.

NORA.
But do you think it would—?

TORVALD.
Just imagine how a guilty man like that has to lie and cheat, all the time and with everybody. What a hypocrite he would have to be; maintaining a façade, keeping a mask on all the time, even with those closest to him: his own wife and kids. And the *kids*—that's the worst part of it, Nora.

NORA.
How so?

TORVALD.
Because this smog of lies infects and rots every last corner of a home. Each breath a child takes in that environment is teeming with the germs of something—so ugly.

She walks closer to him.

NORA.
And you're sure about that?

TORVALD.
Sweetheart, as an attorney I saw it far too often. Almost everyone who was corrupted at an early age has had a liar for a mother.

NORA.
How come it's only the mother?

TORVALD.
It's just that more often than not it's been the mother—although of course a bad father would also have the same outcome. *Every* lawyer knows this, including Nils, and yet, he still chose to poison his own children with lies and deception, and he's been doing so for years. That's why I say he's morally bankrupt.

He holds out his hand to her.

And that's why my sweet little Nora has to promise me never to vouch for him. All right? Let's shake on it. Come on, now! Let's shake on it!

She gives him a somewhat weak handshake. He keeps her hand in his and smiles at her.

And now it's official. I guarantee you, it would've been impossible for me to work with him, anyway. I *literally* get physically sick when I'm around people like him.

NORA takes her hand out of his and goes to the opposite side of the Christmas tree.

NORA.
Have you noticed how hot it got in here? I still have so much to do.

TORVALD goes back to his chair and picks up his documents.

TORVALD.
Yes, and I want to get through some of this work before dinner. And I also need to figure out what to do about your costume, don't think I forgot. I *might* even have something wrapped in gold paper to hang on the tree tonight.

He puts his hand on NORA'S head.

My precious little goldfinch!

He goes into his office and shuts the door. NORA thinks silently for a few seconds.

NORA.
[softly] No, no—it's not true. It's impossible! It *cannot* be possible.

ANNE-MARIE opens the door to the nursery.

ANNE-MARIE.
These little darlings are adorable! They're asking so politely if they can come be with their momma.

NORA.
No, no, no! I can't right now! Please stay with them, Anne-Marie.

ANNE-MARIE.
All right, I'll keep them company.

*She smiles at **NORA** and shuts the door.*

NORA.
[pale with terror] Corrupt our kids? Poison our home? *[A short pause. Then she shakes her head.]* It's not true. There's no possible way that can ever be true.

ACT II

Christmas Day.—The Christmas tree has been moved to the corner by the piano, stripped of its ornaments except for the burnt-down candles on its disheveled branches. **NORA'S** *coat and hat are draped on the sofa. She's alone and walking around nervously. She stops by the sofa and picks up her coat then drops it again.*

NORA.
Someone's coming!

She goes to the door and listens.

No...it's nobody. Of course, no one's coming; it's Christmas Day—probably not tomorrow either. But, maybe—

She opens the door and looks out into the foyer.

No, nothing in the mailbox. Ugh, what am I doing! Of course he's not gonna go through with it. It's not gonna happen; it's impossible!—I have three little kids.

ANNE-MARIE enters from the nursery, carrying a large box.

ANNE-MARIE.
Look what I finally found! Here's that box with all your costumes in it.

NORA.
Thank you, Anne-Marie! Please leave it on the table.

ANNE-MARIE.
[doing so] But they're not in the best shape, I'm afraid.

NORA.
I wish I could just rip them up into a hundred thousand pieces.

ANNE-MARIE.
Oh come on now, they're not *that* bad! It's an easy fix—just have a little patience.

NORA.
Maybe I can go and get Kristine to help.

ANNE-MARIE.
Go out *again*? In this nasty weather? You'll catch cold, love, and get yourself sick!

NORA.
That wouldn't be worst thing that can happen. How are the kids?

ANNE-MARIE.
The poor little sweethearts are playing with their Christmas presents, but—

NORA.
Do they keep asking for me?

ANNE-MARIE.
Well, they're just used to having their momma with them all the time.

NORA.
Yeah, but, Anne-Marie, soon I won't be able to spend as much time with them as I used to.

ANNE-MARIE.
Well…they're just toddlers. It's easy for them to get used to anything.

NORA.
You really think so? Do you think they'd forget their mom if she's gone forever?

ANNE-MARIE.
Good God!—gone forever?

NORA.
Anne-Marie, there's something I've been meaning to ask you for a while—how did you ever have the heart to just leave your own child with strangers?

ANNE-MARIE.
I—had to. It was the only way I could be your nanny.

NORA.
Yeah, but—how did you convince yourself to go through with it?

ANNE-MARIE.
What else would someone in my position have done when a rare good opportunity came along? You don't pass that up. A girl living in poverty, especially one who'd gotten herself into *that* kind of trouble, would be so lucky. —And it wasn't like her so-called father was going to be any help.

NORA.
Do you think she forgot about you?

ANNE-MARIE.
Oh, no, not at all. She actually stayed in touch. She wrote me when she was getting ready for her confirmation at church, and also when she got married.

NORA hugs her.

NORA.
Anne-Marie, you were a great mother to me when I was young.

ANNE-MARIE.
My poor little Nora, to think I was the only mother you had.

NORA.
And if my babies didn't have a mother, I'm sure you'd—Oh, what am I saying!

She lets go of ANNE-MARIE and opens the box.

Why don't you go play with the kids? I have to—. You'll see tomorrow just how exquisite I'll look.

ANNE-MARIE.
I'm sure there won't be anyone at the party who looks more exquisite than you, love.

ANNE-MARIE goes into the nursery. NORA starts to unpack the box, but soon pushes it away from her.

NORA.
If only I could go out…If only I could be sure that no one would come and that nothing would happen in the meantime. Whatever. Don't think about it. No one's coming. Nothing will happen. Exquisite gloves, exquisite gloves! Get out of my head, out of my head! One, two, three, four, five, six—

A sound comes from the foyer.

[With an exasperated scream] Ahh! They're coming—.

She starts walking towards the door, but then stops herself. KRISTINE enters from the foyer, having taken off her coat there.

NORA.
Oh, Kristine, it's you. There's no one else out there, is there? It's so good that you're here!

KRISTINE.
I heard you stopped by my place and asked for me.

NORA.
Yeah, I was just passing by and thought I'd drop in, but you weren't there. Actually, there is something I really do need your help with. Let's sit here on the sofa. So. Tomorrow night there's gonna be a masquerade party at Consul Stenborg's, who lives upstairs, and Torvald wants me to dress up as a Neapolitan village girl, and dance the Tarantella, which I learned in Capri.

KRISTINE.
Oh, I see. So you're gonna put on a whole show, a solo?

NORA.
Yes, Torvald wants me to. Here's the costume. Torvald had it made for me in Italy, but now it's not exactly in the best shape, and I don't have a clue how—

KRISTINE.
Oh, that can be fixed in no time! It just looks like a few things have come a little loose here and there. Got a needle and some thread? That's all we really need.

NORA.
This is so nice of you.

NORA hands KRISTINE some needle and thread, which she then uses to fix the costume.

KRISTINE.
[sewing] So you're gonna be in costume tomorrow, Nora? Tell you what— why don't I drop by for a bit then and see you all dolled up? By the way, I completely forgot to thank you for the cozy evening yesterday.

NORA gets up and walks across the room.

NORA.
Oh, I don't think it was as cozy here yesterday as I would've liked. You should've visited a little sooner, Kristine. Torvald really knows how to make this home feel beautifully exquisite.

KRISTINE.
Well so do you, if you ask me! You are your father's daughter, after all. Incidentally, is Doctor Rank always as gloomy as he was last night?

NORA.
No, it was pretty noticeable yesterday. Then again, he suffers from a very dangerous disease. He has consumption of the spinal cord, poor thing. His father was a disgusting man who had affairs left and right. That's the reason Dr. Rank's been sick since childhood.

KRISTINE drops her sewing.

KRISTINE.
But, Nora, how do you even know about that?

NORA.
Erm…When you have three kids, you get a visit every so often from—from women who know a thing or two about medicine, and they tell you about this and that.

KRISTINE goes back to sewing. There's a short moment of silence.

KRISTINE.
Does Doctor Rank come here every day?

NORA.
Every single day. He's Torvald's closest friend, and a great friend of mine too. He's basically a member of the family.

KRISTINE.
Then, let me ask you—is he totally sincere? I mean…or is he just a people pleaser?

NORA.
Not at all. What makes you think that?

KRISTINE.
When you introduced us yesterday, he said that he heard my name mentioned fairly often in this house; but then I also noticed that your husband didn't have any clue who I was. So how could Doctor Rank—?

NORA.
Yeah, both things can still be true, Kristine. Torvald is so indescribably in love with me that he wants to keep me all to himself, as he likes to say. At first he would get so jealous if I simply mentioned any of my friends back home, so then I avoided doing that. But with Doctor Rank, I just kept talking to him about these things, and he enjoyed listening to me.

KRISTINE.
Listen, Nora. You're still so much like a kid when it comes to a lot of things. I'm a bit older than you and have a tad more experience, so let me tell you this—you have to break off this thing with Doctor Rank.

NORA.
Break off what thing?

KRISTINE.
The "*big*" thing that you—Look, yesterday you mentioned something to me about a rich admirer who was gonna die and leave you money—

NORA.
Yeah, an admirer who doesn't exist, unfortunately! And?

KRISTINE.
Does Doctor Rank have a lot of money?

NORA.
Yes, he does.

KRISTINE.
And no one to take care of?

NORA.
No, no one; but—

KRISTINE.
And he comes here every single day?

NORA.
Yeah, that's what I said.

KRISTINE.
So why would this fine, rich gentleman be so persistent?

NORA.
I'm not following what you're saying.

KRISTINE.
Don't pretend, Nora. Did you think I couldn't figure out who lent you the four thousand eight hundred kroner?

NORA.
Are you out of your mind? How do you even come up with something like that! A close friend of ours, who comes here every day! How awkward of a situation would *that* have been?

KRISTINE.
Then it really wasn't him?

NORA.
No, definitely not. It would never have even crossed my mind. Besides, he had no money to lend back then; he only inherited it afterwards.

KRISTINE.
Well, I think that was lucky for you, my good friend.

NORA.
No, it never would've occurred to me to ask Doctor Rank. Although I'm pretty sure that if I *had* asked him—

KRISTINE.
But of course you wouldn't have.

NORA.
No, of course not. I can't imagine that would've even been necessary. But, still I'm pretty sure that if I spoke to Doctor Rank—

KRISTINE.
Behind your husband's back?

NORA.
I have to get out of the *other* thing, and that's also behind his back. I have to get out of the whole thing.

KRISTINE.
Well, yes, that's what I told you yesterday, but—

NORA.
[paces left and right] A man can fix an issue like this a lot better than a woman—

KRISTINE.
A woman's own husband, yeah.

NORA.
Whatever! *[Standing still.]* When you pay off a debt, you get your bond back, don't you?

KRISTINE.
Yeah, of course.

NORA.
And then you can tear it into a hundred thousand pieces, and burn it up—that disgusting filthy paper!

***KRISTINE** looks hard at **NORA**, puts down her sowing and stands up slowly.*

KRISTINE.
Nora, you're hiding something from me.

NORA.
Do I look like I'm hiding something?

KRISTINE.
Something's happened to you since yesterday morning. Nora, what happened?

***NORA** moves closer to **KRISTINE**.*

NORA.
Kristine! *[Listens.]* Shhh! Torvald just got home. Why don't you go hang out with the kids for a bit? Torvald can't even stand the sight of sewing. Anne-Marie can help you.

***KRISTINE** starts gathering some of the sewing things.*

KRISTINE.
Sure, sounds good—but I'm not going home until I get an answer.

She goes into the nursery, as **TORVALD** *comes in from the foyer.* **NORA** *walks up to* **TORVALD**.

NORA.
Oh, I've been waiting for you, sweetheart.

TORVALD.
Was that the seamstress?

NORA.
No, that was Kristine; she's helping me fix up my costume. You'll see, I'm gonna look exquisite.

TORVALD.
Didn't I tell you I'd come up with a very good idea? Wasn't that nice of me?

NORA.
Absolutely! But don't you think it's nice of me, too, to follow your advice right down to the letter?

TORVALD.
Nice?—to obey your husband? Now, now, you little rascal, I'm sure you didn't mean it that way. But carry on, I'm not gonna bother you. I assume you'll be trying on your costume soon?

NORA.
And you have some work to do, right?

TORVALD.
Yes.

He shows her a bundle of papers.

Look at this. I just got back from the Bank.

TORVALD *turns to go into his office.*

NORA.
Torvald.

TORVALD.
[stops] Yes.

NORA.
If your little kitten asked you for something very, *very* nicely—?

TORVALD.
Yes?

NORA.
Would you do it?

TORVALD.
I think I'd wanna hear what it was first.

NORA.
[with a playful affection] Your kitten would run around and do all her tricks if you were so kind as to do her bidding—

TORVALD.
Why are you talking like that?

NORA.
Your goldfinch would sing in every room, with her melody rising and falling—

TORVALD.
Well, my goldfinch does that now anyway.

NORA.
I'd dress up as an elf-girl and dance for you in the moonlight, Torvald.

TORVALD.
Nora—you wouldn't be talking about what we already discussed this morning, would you?

She moves closer to him.

NORA.
Yes, dearest, I am begging and pleading—

TORVALD.
You really have the nerve to bring that up again?

NORA.
[speaking normally] Oh, honey, you *have* to! You just have to let Nils keep his job the bank.

TORVALD.
Sweetheart, his job is the one that I promised to Kristine.

NORA.
Yes, and you've been very thoughtful about that, but can't you just fire someone else instead?

TORVALD.
Why are you being so incredibly difficult? Just because you gave him your word that you'd vouch for him, I'm expected to—

NORA.
That's not the reason, Torvald. It's for your own good. This guy writes in the worst papers; you said so yourself. He can harm you in unimaginable ways. I'm scared to death of him—

TORVALD.
Oh, ok, now I understand. You're haunted by some old memories.

NORA.
What do you mean?

TORVALD.
Of course you'd be thinking about your father.

NORA.
Yeah—ok. Just remember how those malicious people wrote about him in the papers, and how horribly they smeared his name. I think they would've gotten him fired if the Department hadn't sent you over to look into it, and if you hadn't been so generous and helpful to him.

TORVALD.
My little Nora, there's a big difference between your father and me. Your father was not an unassailable public official. I am, and I hope to stay one for as long as I'm in this job.

NORA.
Oh, who knows what problems evil people can invent? We finally have a chance to live a nice, calm and happy life here in our peaceful, carefree home—you and me and the kids, Torvald! That's why I'm begging you—

TORVALD.
And just by intervening on his behalf, you make it impossible for me to keep him. It's already known at the Bank that I'm planning to fire him. If it gets out that the new Bank Director has been vetoed by his own wife—

NORA.
So what?

TORVALD.
Yeah, so what!—if only this stubborn little girl can get her way! Why don't I just go and make myself look ridiculous in front of my whole staff while I'm at it? Let people know how easily I'm swayed by all kinds of external influence. I'd feel the heat pretty quick, I can tell you that much! But also, there's one thing that makes it pretty impossible for me to keep Nils at the Bank so long as I'm the director.

NORA.
And what's that?

TORVALD.
Sure, if it comes down to it, I could overlook his moral deficits—

NORA.
Sure you can—can't you?

TORVALD.
And I hear he's pretty good at his job, too. But I've known him since we were practically kids. It was one of those foolish friendships that you're embarrassed about later in life. At one point, I hate to say it, we had even been somewhat close. And this guy, who has no tact or sense of discipline, loves to play it up *especially* when others are around. Oh, yes, he thinks it entitles him to be completely informal around me, and every minute it's "my buddy Torvald this" and "My pal Torvald that." It's so embarrassing. He would make my job at the Bank completely unbearable.

NORA.
Torvald, you can't be serious?

TORVALD.
Oh? Why not?

NORA.
Because that's such a petty thing to be upset about.

TORVALD.
What're you saying? Petty? You think *I'm* petty?

NORA.
No, honey, just the opposite—and it's exactly why—

TORVALD.
That's what it sounded like. You said my concerns are petty, so I guess that makes me petty, too. Petty! Ok—This has to end now.

He marches to the foyer and calls out.

Helena!

NORA.
What're you doing?

TORVALD *looks through his papers as* **HELENA** *enters.*

TORVALD.
Settling this thing. *[To **HELENA**]* Here, take this letter and go downstairs

immediately. Grab a courier and tell him to deliver it. Quickly! The address is on it. Here's some money.

HELENA.
Sure thing, Mr. Helmer

She exits with the letter and money, her footsteps quickly fading away.
TORVALD picks up the rest of his papers and turns to his wife triumphantly.

TORVALD.
Well, that's that, little Miss Obstinate.

NORA.
[breathlessly] Torvald—what was in that letter?

TORVALD.
Nils' termination.

NORA.
Call her back, Torvald! There's still time. Torvald, call her back! Do it for me—for yourself—for your kids! Are you even listening to me, Torvald? Call her back! You don't know what that letter can bring down on all of us.

TORVALD.
Too late.

NORA.
Yeah…too late.

TORVALD.
Sweetheart, I can excuse the anxiety you're going through, even though it's basically an insult to me. Yes, it is! Don't you think it's an insult to assume that I would be scared of a worthless lawyer's revenge? But I forgive you anyway, because, if you think about it, it's actually a beautiful testament to your love for me.

He hugs her.

And that's just how it should be, my own darling Nora. Come what may. If it really comes to it, you can be sure that I have both strength and courage. You'll see that I'm man enough to bear any and all burdens.

NORA.
[Terrified] What do you mean by that?

TORVALD.
I mean *any* and *all*—

NORA.
[firmly] No, you'll never, ever have to do that.

TORVALD.
All right. Then we'll share the burden, Nora, as husband and wife. That's how it should be anyway.

He caresses her face.

Feel better now? Oh, hey, now, come on!—Eyes like a terrified dove. No need for that! This is just pure fantasy!—Now, you should go run through the Tarantella and rehearse with your tambourine. I'm gonna go into my inner office and shut both doors, that way I won't hear a thing. You can make as much noise as you like. And when Rank gets here, tell him where he can find me.

TORVALD nods to her, takes his papers, goes into his office, and shuts the door. NORA, bewildered with anxiety, stands as if nailed to the floor, and whispers to herself.

NORA.
He was ready to do it. He's gonna do it. He will do it, despite everything.— No, not that! Never, never! Anything's better than that! A rescue! A way out!

The doorbell rings.

Doctor Rank! Anything's better than that—anything, whatever it takes!

She puts her hands over her face, pulls herself together, goes to the door and opens it. RANK is standing in the foyer, hanging up his coat. The sun is setting and, as they speak, the room begins to get dark.

Hello, Doctor Rank. Did Helena let you in? I knew it was you as soon as the doorbell rang. But Torvald can't see you just yet. I think he's busy with something.

RANK.
And you?

NORA brings him in and shuts the door after him.

NORA.
Oh, you know me well enough to know I always have time for you.

RANK.
Thank you. I'll take as much of it for as long as I can.

NORA.
What do you mean by that? For as long as you can?

RANK.
Does that worry you?

NORA.
It's just such an odd expression. Is something gonna happen?

RANK.
Nothing more than what I've already been prepared for. But I definitely didn't expect it to happen so soon.

She grips his arm tightly

NORA.
What've you heard? Doctor Rank, you have to tell me.

He goes over by the fireplace and sits down. She follows him.

RANK.
It's all downhill for me, I'm afraid. And there's nothing I can do about it.

NORA.
[with a sigh of relief] Oh, this is about you.

RANK.
Who else? There's no point in lying to myself. I'm the most miserable of all my patients, Nora. The past few days I've taken a full account of my health. Bankrupt! By the end of the month I'll probably be six feet under rotting in a cemetery.

NORA.
Doctor Rank, that's such an ugly thing to say!

RANK.
The whole damn thing is ugly. And worst of all is that there's a whole lot more ugliness left to come. There's only one medical test I still need to do. When that's done, I'll know how rapidly my condition will deteriorate and when my final hours will roughly come. There's something I need to tell you. Torvald, in his genteel sensibilities, has such a distinct aversion to anything he considers ugly; I don't want him there by my side when—

NORA.
Oh, Doctor Rank—

RANK.
I *don't* want him there. Under any circumstances. My door will be closed to him. As soon as I'm sure that the worst's finally come, I'll send you my business card with a black cross on it, and then you'll know that my "abomination of desolation" has begun.

NORA.
You're being so ridiculous today. And here I was hoping you'd be in a really good mood.

RANK.
With death knocking on my door?—And to have to pay this price for another man's sin. Is there any justice in that? It seems in every family, one way or another, there's this relentless divine retribution being executed—

NORA.
[putting her hands over her ears] Oh, stop it! Happy thoughts! Happy thoughts!

RANK.
Now, you can't help but laugh at the whole thing, really. My poor innocent spine's forced to suffer for all the good times my father had as a lieutenant.

NORA.
I guess he did have a weakness for foie gras, didn't he?

RANK.
Yes, and truffles.

NORA.
Truffles, yes. And oysters too, I think?

RANK.
Oh, yes, oysters, of course, goes without saying.

NORA.
And then all that port and champagne. It's so sad all these delicacies would impact the spine like that.

RANK.
Sadder, even, to impact the unfortunate spine of someone who hasn't had the pleasure of enjoying them.

NORA.
Yes, that's the saddest part of it all.

RANK.
[looking at NORA intently] Hmm!—

NORA.
[after a short pause] Why did you smile?

RANK.
No, it was you who laughed.

NORA.
No, it was *you* who smiled, Doctor Rank!

RANK.
You're more of a troublemaker than I thought.

NORA.
I *have* been thinking about getting into a little trouble today.

RANK.
Seems like it.

She puts both her hands on his shoulders.

NORA.
Oh, Doctor Rank—you can't go and die on us like that!

RANK.
Eh, you'd get over it quickly. Out of sight, out of mind.

NORA.
[looking at him anxiously] You really believe that?

RANK.
People make new connections, and then—

NORA.
Who's making new connections?

RANK.
You and Torvald—after I'm gone. I think you already have a head start on that, actually. What was this Kristine Linde doing here last night?

NORA.
Oh, come on now!— you're not actually jealous of her?

RANK.
Yes, I am. She'll be my replacement. When I'm gone, this woman might—

NORA.
Shhh! don't talk so loud! She's in the next room.

RANK.
Today, too? See what I mean?

NORA.
She only stopped by to fix my costume. Oh my God, you're being so ridiculous! Be nice, now, Doctor Rank! Tomorrow, you'll get to see how well I can dance, and you can even pretend that I'm doing it just for you— and for Torvald too, of course.

She takes various things out of the costume box.

Doctor Rank, come here and sit down, I want to show you something.

RANK.
[sitting down] What is it?

NORA.
Would you look at these!

RANK.
Silk stockings?

NORA.
Nude silk stockings! Aren't they just *exquisite*? Well, it's dark in here right now, so you can't tell, but *tomorrow*—. No, no, I guess you wouldn't be able to, then, either. You'd only be allowed to see up to here…Ok, fine, I *might* let you sneak a peek a little higher.

RANK.
Hmm!—

NORA.
Why the judgmental look? You don't think they'll fit me?

RANK.
I have no way of forming an accurate opinion about that.

She looks at him for a brief moment.

NORA.
[Jokingly] Shame on you!

***NORA** hits him lightly on the ear with her stockings.*

Take that!

She folds them up and throws them in the box.

RANK.
And what other wonders can I look forward to seeing tomorrow?

NORA.
Not a single thing more, since you've been so naughty!

She looks through other things in the box while humming to herself.

RANK.
[after a short silence] You know, when I'm sitting here, talking to you as intimately as we have been, I can't imagine….I just can't imagine what would've happened to me if I'd never come to this house.

NORA.
[smiling] Yes, I think you've felt right at home here with us.

RANK.
[in a lower voice, looking straight in front of him] And then having to leave it all—

NORA.
Oh hush, you're not going anywhere.

RANK.
[continuing] —without being able to leave behind a small token of my gratitude, not even a brief sense of loss—nothing except an empty space that's easily filled by the first person to come along.

NORA.
What if I asked you for—? Never mind!

RANK.
For what?

NORA.
For a big testament to your friendship—

RANK.
Yes?

NORA.
I mean, it would be a *very* big favor—

RANK.
Would you please just make me happy this one time?

NORA.
But you don't even know what the favor is yet.

RANK.
All right, then tell me.

NORA.
I really can't, Doctor Rank. It's totally unreasonable! We're talking advice, and help, and a *huge* favor—

RANK.
Well, I can't imagine what you mean, but you can still tell me. Do you trust me?

NORA.
More than anyone else, I think. I know that you're my closest and best friend. That's why I *want* to tell you. Well, Doctor Rank, it's something you have

to help me prevent. You know how deeply, how enormously Torvald loves me. He would risk his own life for me—

RANK.
[leaning towards her] Do you think he's the only one—?

NORA.
[slightly startled] The only one—?

RANK.
—Who'd risk his own life for you?

NORA.
[sadly] I see.

RANK.
I swore to myself that I'd let you know before I died. There wouldn't've been a better time than the present. So now you know that, Nora. And now you also *know* that you can trust me more than you can trust anybody else.

NORA stands, deliberately and quietly

NORA.
I have to go.

RANK makes room for her to pass him, but remains seated

RANK.
Nora!

She goes towards the foyer and calls out.

NORA.
Helena, can you please bring in the lamp.

She turns and goes over to the fireplace.

Doctor Rank, that was really horrible of you.

RANK.
To have loved you as much as anybody else? Was that really horrible?

NORA.
No, but to tell me about it…That wasn't necessary at all—

RANK.
What do you mean? Did you *know*—?

HELENA enters with a lamp. She pretends not to notice the palpably awkward atmosphere, inadvertently making it more awkward for everyone.

She tries to find a place to put the lamp and decides on the table. She sets it there and backs out of the room. After a moment:

Nora—did you know?

NORA.
Oh, how would I know if I knew or didn't know? I really can't say—to think you could be so awkward, Doctor Rank! Everything was going great.

RANK.
Well, at least you now know that I'm at your disposal, body and soul. So won't you tell me what you need?

NORA.
[looking at him] After *that*?

RANK.
I'm begging you, just tell me what you need.

NORA.
I can't tell you anything now.

RANK.
Yes, please. You shouldn't punish me like this. Let me help you in any way possible.

NORA.
You can't do anything for me now. Besides, I don't really need help anyway. You'll see, it's all just been in my head. It really, really has!

She sits down in the rocking-chair, and looks at him with a smile.

You really are a handsome gentleman, Doctor Rank!—don't you feel ashamed of yourself, now that there's some light in the room?

RANK.
No, not really. But maybe I should go away—forever?

NORA.
Oh, stop it. You're gonna keep coming here just as much as before. You know as well as I do that Torvald can't go on without you.

RANK.
Yes, and you?

NORA.
Oh, I always think it's much more entertaining when you're around.

RANK.
And that's exactly what lured me down this path. You're such an enigma to

me. I often felt as if you'd almost like to be with me as much as you would with Torvald.

NORA.
Well—you see, there are those you love the most, and others you'd *almost* like to be with.

RANK.
Yes, there's some truth to that.

NORA.
When I still lived back home, of course I loved dad the most. But I always thought it was a lot more fun to sneak down to the maids' room, because they never lectured me or preached at me at all, and always talked about the most fun things.

RANK.
I see—so I'm the maids' replacement.

NORA.
Doctor Rank, you know that's not what I meant at all. But I'm sure you can appreciate how living with Torvald is, in a way, like living with my father—

HELENA enters from the foyer looking a bit uncomfortable.

HELENA.
Mrs. Helmer.

She whispers to NORA and hands her a card. NORA glances at it and quickly puts it in her pocket.

RANK.
Is there something wrong?

NORA.
No, no, not at all. It's just um—it's my new costume—

RANK.
What? You said your costume's right in there.

NORA.
Oh, yes, *that* one—but this is a different one. I ordered it. Torvald can't know that I—

RANK.
Ahh! So *that* was the big secret.

NORA.
Yeah, sure. Why don't you go see him? He locked himself up in his inner office. Please keep him busy as long as—

RANK.
Calm down, don't worry; I won't let him escape.
He goes into ***TORVALD'S*** *office.*

NORA.
*[to **HELENA**]* So he's waiting in the kitchen?

HELENA.
Yes. He came up the backstairs—

NORA.
And you told him someone was already here?

HELENA.
Yes, but it made no difference.

NORA.
He won't just go away?

HELENA.
No. He says he's not leaving until he's had a nice long chat with you. His words.

NORA.
Fine, tell him to come in—but quietly. Helena, you *cannot* say anything about this to anyone. It's a surprise for my husband.

HELENA.
A surprise, sure, yes. I understand.

She goes out through the foyer and into the kitchen. ***NORA*** *paces back and forth.*

NORA.
This is happening! This is really happening! No, no, no, it can't happen—it *won't* happen!

She locks the door to ***TORVALD'S*** *office.* ***HELENA*** *ushers* ***NILS*** *in and shuts the door after him.* ***NORA*** *marches towards him.*

Be quiet—my husband's home.

NILS.
Doesn't matter.

NORA.
What do you want from me?

NILS.
An explanation, to start.

NORA.
Well, hurry up. What is it?

NILS.
You probably know that I received my dismissal notice.

NORA.
I couldn't stop it, Nils. I fought for you as hard as I could, but it made no difference.

NILS.
Does your husband have so little love for you, then? I mean, he is aware of what I can do to you, but he still—

NORA.
Why would you assume he knows about any of that?

NILS.
I didn't assume anything. It just wouldn't be like my good buddy Torvald to *actually* behave like a real man—

NORA.
Nils, I *demand* you show a little respect for my husband.

NILS.
Well, yes—that's all the respect he deserves. But since you've obviously been so anxious about keeping this whole thing a secret, would it be bold of me to assume that, since our last chat, you've gained a bit more insight into the legal consequences of your actions?

NORA.
More than you could ever teach me.

NILS.
Yeah, such a terrible lawyer, as you said.

NORA.
What is it you want from me?

NILS.
Only to see how you're doing! I've actually been thinking about you all day. You may not know this, Nora, but a debt-collector, a lawyer, a—you now, someone like me—even I have that little thing people call a heart.

NORA.
Prove it, then! Think about my little kids.

NILS.
Have you and your husband ever thought about mine? But never mind about

that. I just wanted to tell you that you don't need to take this problem so seriously. First of all, I won't be pressing charges.

NORA.
No, of course not. I was sure you wouldn't.

NILS.
The whole thing can be resolved peacefully. There's no reason why anyone would have to know anything about it. We'll just keep it between the three of us.

NORA.
My husband can't ever know anything about it.

NILS.
And just how're you gonna prevent that? Can *you* pay the balance that you still owe?

NORA.
No, not at the moment.

NILS.
Or maybe you've found a quick and easy way to make money?

NORA.
Not one that I'm willing to use.

NILS.
Well, it wouldn't've made a difference anyway. You can stand here right now with a pile of cash in your hand, and I still wouldn't give you your bond back.

NORA.
Then explain to me why you want it so much.

NILS.
Just to have it—keep it safe. No one who's not involved will ever even see it. So, if you're going around trying to come up with some sort of desperate solution—

NORA.
I am.

NILS.
—maybe debating running away from home—

NORA.
I am!

NILS.
—or possibly considering something even worse—

NORA.
How would you know?

NILS.
—then cut it out.

NORA.
How would you know that I had thought about it?

NILS.
Most of us think about it at first. I thought about it, too. But I didn't have the guts—

NORA.
[faintly] I don't either.

NILS.
[relieved] No, you don't—you don't have the guts for it, do you? And what a stupid mistake *that* would've been, anyway, when you could've just waited for the domestic storm to pass—. I have a letter for your husband in my pocket.

NORA.
Telling him everything?

NILS.
As delicately as I possibly could.

NORA.
[quickly] He can't get that letter. Rip it up, just rip it up. I'll find a way to get you the money.

NILS.
Sorry, Nora, but I'm pretty sure I already said that—

NORA.
Ugh, I'm not talking about what I owe you. Tell me how much money you plan on getting from my husband, and I'll get it for you instead.

NILS.
I'm not asking your husband for money.

NORA.
What do you want, then?

NILS.
I wanna get back on my feet, Nora; to move up in this life; and that's

something he can help me with. For the past year and a half I stayed completely out of trouble, even when I had to make it through some pretty miserable situations. I was actually happy to climb my way up step by step. Now I'm being pushed down again, but this time I'm not gonna simply settle for the same old thing. This time I wanna move *up* in life, you hear me? I wanna work at the Bank again, but in a higher position. Your husband needs to create that position for me—

NORA.
He'll never do that!

NILS.
He will. I know him. He won't even grumble about it. And as soon as I'm back in there again, you'll see! It won't even be a year before I'm his right hand man. And then it'll be Nils Krogstad, and not Torvald Helmer, who runs the Commercial Bank.

NORA.
I'd die before I let that happen.

NILS.
Huh, so you're saying you'd actually—?

NORA.
I have the guts for it now.

NILS.
Oh, please, look at you. A delicate, pampered flower like you could never—

NORA.
Well, you'll see.

NILS.
How? Under the ice, maybe? Drown in the cold, black water? And then float up in the spring, all ugly and unrecognizable, with your filthy hair and—

NORA.
You don't scare me.

NILS.
Neither do you. People don't do things like that, Nora. Besides, what difference would that make? I'd have him in my pocket either way.

NORA.
After I'm dead? You still think you could—

NILS.
You're forgetting that, at that point, I would have total control of your reputation. You wouldn't even be there to defend yourself.

NORA stands speechless, looking at him for a moment.

Well, now that I've warned you…Don't go doing anything stupid. I'll be expecting to hear from Torvald as soon as he reads my letter. Just remember, it was your husband who forced me to do this. I'll never forgive him for that. Goodbye, Nora.

He exit through the foyer and closes the door after himself. **NORA** *goes to the door, cracks it open, and listens.*

NORA.
He's leaving. Doesn't sound like he's putting the letter in the box. No, that wouldn't make any sense!

She slowly opens the door wider, trying to catch sight of him.

What? He's just standing in front of the mailbox. He's not even going downstairs. Did he change his mind? Could he—?

We hear the sound of a letter dropping into the mailbox. His footsteps fade away as he goes downstairs. With a stifled cry, **NORA** *runs across the room. A short pause.*

NORA.
In the mailbox.

She treads nervously back to the open door.

There it is—Torvald, Torvald, there's no way out of this now!

KRISTINE *comes in from the nursery, carrying* **NORA'S** *costume.*

KRISTINE.
Well, looks like it's all fixed up now. You wanna try it on—?

NORA.
[in a hoarse whisper] Kristine, come here.

KRISTINE *throws the costume down on the sofa.*

KRISTINE.
What's wrong? You look a little nauseous!

NORA.
Come here. Do you see that letter? Through the glass in the mailbox?

KRISTINE.
Yeah, I see it.

NORA.
That letter is from Nils Krogstad.

KRISTINE.
Nora—so it was Nils who lent you the money?!

NORA.
Yes, and now Torvald's gonna find out about it.

KRISTINE.
Believe me, Nora, that's the best thing for both of you.

NORA.
There's more to it than that. I forged a signature.

KRISTINE.
You what?

NORA.
I'm only telling *you* this, Kristine—I need you to be my witness.

KRISTINE.
Your witness? What would that involve exactly—?

NORA.
If I go crazy—and at this point it could really happen—

KRISTINE.
Nora!

NORA.
Or if something else happens to me—something that keeps me from being here—

KRISTINE.
Nora—honey, you're clearly out of your mind!

NORA.
There's a possibility that someone *else* might try to take all the blame, if you know what I mean—?

KRISTINE.
Yes, yes—but why would you think—?

NORA.
If that happens, Kristine, I need you to be my witness that it's *not* true. And I'm not out of my mind. I'm "of perfectly sound mind and body," and I'm

telling you that no one else knew *anything* about what I did. I did it totally on my own. Remember that.

KRISTINE.
I will. But I don't understand why—

NORA.
Don't you get it? *The Divine* is finally gonna happen!

KRISTINE.
The Divine?

NORA.
Yes, *the Divine*!—But it's also awful, Kristine! It can't happen, no matter what.

KRISTINE.
I'll go right now and have a talk with Nils.

NORA.
No, don't go there, he'll only hurt you.

KRISTINE.
There was a time when he would've done anything for me.

NORA.
Nils?

KRISTINE.
Where does he live?

NORA.
How should I know—? Oh, yes *[feeling in her pocket]*, there's his card. But the letter, Kristine, the letter—!

TORVALD *knocks on the locked door of his office.*

TORVALD.
[off] Nora? Nora!

NORA.
[screams] What is it? What do you want?

TORVALD.
[off] Don't worry, sweetheart. We're not barging in. You locked the door. Are you trying on your costume?

NORA.
Yes…Yes I am. I'm gonna look so beautiful, Torvald.

KRISTINE.
[who has read the card] Looks like he lives right around the corner.

NORA.
Yes, but it won't make any difference. It's hopeless. His letter's sitting right there in the mailbox.

KRISTINE.
And only your husband has the key?

NORA.
Yes, always.

KRISTINE.
Nils can ask for his letter back unread, he just needs an excuse—

NORA.
But this is the time Torvald usually checks—

KRISTINE.
Stall. I'll come back as soon as I can.

She rushes out through the foyer. **NORA** *goes to* **TORVALD'S** *door, unlocks it, and peeks in.*

NORA.
Torvald!

TORVALD.
[off] Well? Am I finally allowed to go into my own living room? Come on, Rank, now we'll finally get to see—

He stops n the doorway with **RANK** *right behind him.*

What's this?

NORA.
What's what, honey?

TORVALD.
Rank had me thinking I'd get to witness a remarkable transformation.

RANK.
[at the door] That's what I thought, but I guess I was wrong.

NORA.
Yeah, well, no one's witnessing any remarkable transformations until tomorrow.

TORVALD.
Sweetheart, you look so exhausted. Have you been rehearsing a little too hard?

NORA.
No, actually I haven't gotten a chance to rehearse at all.

TORVALD.
Well, you're gonna *have* to—

NORA.
Yes, yes, I will, Torvald. But you know me, I can't do *anything* without your help; I totally forgot the whole dance.

TORVALD.
Oh, well, I guess I can refresh your memory.

NORA.
Yes, *please* help me, Torvald. Promise you will? I'm just so nervous about it—all those people—. You're gonna have to give up your *whole* evening. Not a single second of work. Promise, honey?

TORVALD.
Ok, I promise. This evening I'm totally at your disposal, you helpless little thing. Ah, by the way, I just need to check—

He walks towards the foyer.

NORA.
What're you doing?

TORVALD.
Just checking the mail.

NORA.
No, no! Don't do that, Torvald!

TORVALD.
Why not?

NORA.
Oh, Torvald, don't bother. There's nothing there.

TORVALD.
I'll just take a quick look.

He turns to go to the mailbox. **NORA** *runs to the piano and starts playing the first few bars of the Tarantella.* **TORVALD** *stops at the door and turns towards her.*

NORA.
I can't dance tomorrow if I don't rehearse with you.

TORVALD.
[going up to her] Are you really *that* anxious about it, sweetheart?

NORA.
Yes, *so* anxious. Let's rehearse right now! We have some time before dinner. Sit down and play for me, honey. Guide and correct me like you always do.

TORVALD.
I'd be more than happy to, if that's really what you want.

He sits down at the piano. **NORA** *takes a tambourine and a colorful fringed shawl out of the costume box. She hastily drapes it around her shoulders and springs to the middle of the room.*

NORA.
Now play for me! I wanna dance!

TORVALD *plays and* **NORA** *dances as* **RANK** *stands by the piano and watches. She dances around wildly, frantically, desperately.* **TORVALD** *hesitates in his playing but continues.*

TORVALD.
[as he plays] Slow down, not so fast!

NORA.
I don't know how else to do it.

TORVALD.
Not so frantically, Nora!

NORA.
But that's how it needs to be.

TORVALD *stops playing.*

TORVALD.
No, no—that's all wrong.

NORA *laughs and swings the tambourine around.*

NORA.
Told you so!

RANK.
Let me play for her.

TORVALD.
Yes, please. I can correct her mistakes better that way.

TORVALD stands up and RANK takes his place at the piano and plays. NORA'S dance grows more and more frantic. TORVALD stands by the fireplace, and, as NORA dances, he gives her frequent instructions, but she doesn't seem to hear him. The adornments in her hair fly off, but she pays no attention to them. She just goes on dancing. KRISTINE enters and stands at the door, shocked at what she's witnessing. NORA sees her but keeps on dancing.

NORA.
[as she dances] Isn't this fun, Kristine?

TORVALD.
Nora, sweetheart, it looks like you're dancing as if your life depends on it.

NORA.
It does, doesn't it?

TORVALD.
Stop, Rank, this is insane. Stop, please!

RANK stops playing, and NORA abruptly stands still. TORVALD marches up to her.

I don't believe this. You forgot everything I taught you.

She tosses the tambourine away.

NORA.
Told you so!

TORVALD.
You need *a lot* of coaching.

NORA.
Yeah, I do, don't I? You're gonna have work with me right up to the last minute. Promise me, Torvald!

TORVALD.
You can count on me.

NORA.
You're not allowed to think of anything except me, today *and* tomorrow. You can't read a single letter—in fact, you don't even need to open the mailbox at all—

TORVALD.
Ah, I see…you're still afraid of that guy—

NORA.
Yes. Yes, I am.

TORVALD.
Nora, I can see it in your eyes. There's a letter in there from him, isn't there?

NORA.
I don't know; maybe; but you shouldn't be reading anything from him, anyway. I don't want anything ugly to come between us, at least until the party's over.

RANK.
*[whispers to **TORVALD**]* It would really be easier if you just went along with it.

***TORVALD** takes **NORA** in his arms.*

TORVALD.
Fine, the child can have her way. But tomorrow night, after the party—

NORA.
Then you'll be free.

***HELENA** appears in the foyer doorway.*

HELENA.
Dinner is served.

NORA.
We'll have champagne, Helena.

HELENA.
Of course, Mrs. Helmer.

She heads to the kitchen.

TORVALD.
Hey, now!—are we turning this dinner into a party?

NORA.
Yes, a champagne party until dawn. *[Calls out to **HELENA**.]* And a couple of macaroons, Helena—just for tonight!

TORVALD.
Let's not get too crazy, now! Can I just get my own little goldfinch back?

NORA.
Don't worry, you will. But you go on ahead, and you too, Doctor Rank. Kristine, would you mind helping me fix my hair first?

RANK.
[whispers to **TORVALD** *as they go out]* Do you think there's something—I mean, is she *expecting* something?

TORVALD.
No, not at all. It's just this childish anxiety I told you about.

They go out to the dining room.

NORA.
So?

KRISTINE.
Went outta town.

NORA.
I figured. I saw it in your eyes.

KRISTINE.
He'll be back tomorrow evening, though. I left him a note.

NORA.
You shouldn't have; no point in trying to prevent anything. Actually, it's a pleasure to just sit here and wait for the Divine to happen.

KRISTINE.
What exactly is this "Divine" you're waiting for?

NORA.
You wouldn't get it. Please, go join them. I'll be right there.

KRISTINE *goes into the dining room.* **NORA** *stands still for a moment, regaining her composure, and then checks her watch.*

Five o'clock. Seven hours until midnight; and then another twenty-four after that. Then the dance'll be over. Twenty-four plus seven. That's thirty-one hours left to live.

TORVALD.
[from the doorway] Where's my little goldfinch?

As though nothing had happened, she runs to him with open arms.

NORA.
Here she is!

ACT III

The same room, the next night. The table's been moved to the middle of the room, with chairs all around it. The door to the foyer is open. Faint sounds of dance music are heard from upstairs. **KRISTINE** *is sitting at the table absentmindedly flipping through the pages of a book; she tries to read, but can't focus. She puts down the book, picks up her knitting, and then sets it down after a stitch or two. Every now and then she listens closely for a sound to come from the front door. After a moment, she checks her watch.*

KRISTINE.
Still not here—and time's running out. If he doesn't—. *[Listens again.]* Good, sounds like he made it.

She goes into the foyer, cautiously opens the front door and hears the sound of light footsteps coming up the stairs. She whispers.

Come on in. There's no one here.

NILS.
[at the door] I found a note from you at home. What's this about?

KRISTINE.
We need to have a talk.

NILS.
Really? And do we need to have it *here*?

KRISTINE.
We can't where I'm staying; my room doesn't have a private entrance. Come in, we're all alone. The maid's sleeping, and the Helmers are upstairs at a party.

NILS.
[coming into the room] So they're really partying tonight? Seriously?

KRISTINE.
Yeah, why not?

NILS.
You're right—why not?

KRISTINE.
So, then, let's talk.

NILS.
What's there even left for us to talk about?

KRISTINE.
There's a lot left for us to talk about.

NILS.
I wouldn't've thought so.

KRISTINE.
No, that's because you never understood me properly.

NILS.
Oh, ok, was there anything else to understand, besides the same old story? A cruel woman ditches a man when a more lucrative prospect shows up.

KRISTINE.
You really think I'm cruel? Like it was so easy for me to break up with you?

NILS.
Wasn't it?

KRISTINE.
Nils, do you honestly believe that?

NILS.
Well if that's not the case, then why did you write all those awful things to me back then?

KRISTINE.
I didn't have a choice. When I *had* to break things off with you, I also had make sure you had no feelings left for me. None.

NILS.
[Clenching his fist] Wow, ok. So that whole thing—it's only ever been about the money!

KRISTINE.
I had to provide for a helpless mother and two little boys, don't you forget that. We couldn't wait for you, Nils. Your future wasn't exactly looking very bright at the time.

NILS.
Maybe it wasn't, but you still had *no right* to just throw me away like that— not for *anybody's* sake.

KRISTINE.
Yeah, no…maybe. There were a lot of times when I asked myself if I really did have that right.

NILS.
[more gently, after composing himself] When I lost you, it felt like the earth

had gone out from under me. Now look at me—I'm just a castaway hanging on to the wreck.

KRISTINE.
Maybe there's a lifeboat on the way.

NILS.
There was…but then you stopped it.

KRISTINE.
I didn't know, Nils, it's not like I did this on purpose. I only found out today that I was taking over *your* job.

NILS.
Ok, I'll take your word for it. But now that you *do* know, would you quit?

KRISTINE.
No. It wouldn't do you any good anyway.

NILS.
Any good anyway—I would've done it for you.

KRISTINE.
Well, I learned to be a little more practical, Nils. Life, and a harsh, bitter reality taught me that.

NILS.
And life's taught me not trust some empty words.

KRISTINE.
Then life's taught you something very practical.

They stand tensely in their discomfort for a few seconds.

What about actions?

NILS.
What do you mean?

KRISTINE.
You said you were just a castaway hanging on to the wreck.

NILS.
I have my reasons.

KRISTINE.
Well, I'm a castaway hanging on to the wreck, too—I have nobody. No one to take care of. No one to mourn.

NILS.
That was your own choice.

KRISTINE.
I had *no other choice.*

NILS.
Ok, fine, you had no choice.

A few seconds of awkward silence.

What now?

KRISTINE.
Nils, what if there's a way for the two castaways to reach out to each other?

NILS.
What're you saying?

KRISTINE.
That they'd have a better chance of surviving together than on their own.

NILS.
Kristine!

KRISTINE.
Why do you think I came to this town?

NILS.
What, are you saying I factored into that decision?

KRISTINE.
I *have* to work, Nils! I don't think I can even stand this life if I didn't. I've always worked. All my life, and as far back as can I remember. And it has been my greatest and only joy. But, like I said, I'm now all alone in this world and I'm left feeling empty and abandoned. I don't get any satisfaction out of working for myself, Nils. Give me something… some*one* to work for.

NILS.
I don't buy that. Only a woman's overbearing sense of altruism would drive her to sacrifice herself like this.

KRISTINE.
When have I ever been overbearing?

NILS.
Is this what you *really* want? Let me ask you—are you even aware of my past?

KRISTINE.
Yes.

NILS.
And you know what they think of me around here?

KRISTINE.
The way you were talking earlier, it sounded like you think you would've turned out differently if we had stayed together.

NILS.
I *know* that, absolutely.

KRISTINE.
That can still happen, though, can't it?

NILS.
Kristine, are you actually being serious?

He looks at her. She looks back at him. He sighs.

Yeah. I can tell from your eyes. But with everything I've been going through, I don't know if you even wanna risk—

KRISTINE.
I want to be a mother, and your kids need one. We both need each other, Nils. I have faith in you—maybe together we can handle anything.

He holds her hands.

NILS.
Thank you, Kristine. Really, thank you! Maybe now I can finally have a chance to get things back on track. But what about—

The music heard from upstairs has changed to the Tarantella.

KRISTINE.
[listening] Shh! The Tarantella's started! You have to go!

NILS.
Why? What's happening?

KRISTINE.
You hear that? When *that's* over, it'll only be matter of minutes before they're back.

NILS.
Ok, ok, I'll go. Not that it makes any difference. You don't even know what I've already done to them, do you?

KRISTINE.
Yes, I know all about that.

NILS.
And you're *sure* you still want to—?

KRISTINE.
I understand very well how far a man like you is willing to go when he's desperate.

NILS.
I wish I could undo what I did.

KRISTINE.
I mean, you *can*. Your letter's still in the mailbox.

NILS.
Are you sure?

KRISTINE.
Yes, but I think—

NILS.
[looking at her suspiciously] Wait, is that what this is about?—you're just trying to save your friend, no matter what? Just, please, tell me. Is that it?

KRISTINE.
Nils, those who've sold themselves off once for the benefit of someone else would never do it twice.

NILS.
Then I'll just ask for my letter back.

KRISTINE.
No, no.

NILS.
Why not? I can wait here until Torvald comes down. I'll tell him that he has to give it back to me—that it was just a gut reaction to him firing me and now I'm too embarrassed for him to read it—

KRISTINE.
No, Nils, you shouldn't ask for your letter back.

NILS.
Isn't that exactly why you wanted me to meet you *here*?

KRISTINE.
In a moment of panic, yes. But it's been a whole day since, and honestly you wouldn't even believe all the things I witnessed here in that time. Torvald *needs* to know all of it. This unfortunate secret *has* to be brought to light and

there *must* be a complete and total understanding between them. It's impossible to keep up with all these secrets and lies and excuses.

NILS.
As long as you're willing to take that risk—But there's at least one thing I *can* do, I just have to do it now.

KRISTINE *notices that the Tarantella music coming from upstairs has stopped.*

KRISTINE.
Hurry up and go! The dance just ended. It's not safe here anymore.

NILS.
I'll wait for you downstairs.

KRISTINE.
Yes. You'll have to walk me home, you know.

NILS.
Kristine, this is the happiest I've ever been in all my life!

He goes through the foyer and out the front door, leaving the door to the foyer open behind him. ***KRISTINE*** *tidies up around the room and grabs her coat.*

KRISTINE.
What a difference! God, what a difference! Someone to care for, to live for—a home to fill with light and warmth and comfort. There's just one more thing left to do. I wish they'd hurry up—*[Listens.]* And here they are.

She throws on her coat while ***TORVALD*** *and* ***NORA'S*** *voices are heard outside the door. A key is turned, and* ***TORVALD*** *leads* ***NORA*** *inside almost by force. She's in her Tarantella costume with a large shawl draped over her shoulders; he's in evening dress with a black domino cloak on top, which had come undone.* ***NORA*** *stands back by the door, reluctant to come inside.*

NORA.
No, no, no!—I don't wanna go home yet. I wanna go back upstairs! I don't wanna leave so early.

TORVALD.
But Nora, darling—

NORA.
I'm begging you, Torvald—please, please—just one more hour.

TORVALD.
Not one more minute, sweetheart. You know that was our deal. Come now, into the living room, you'll catch a cold standing there.

In spite of her resistance, **TORVLAD** *leads her gently into the room, neither having noticed* **KRISTINE** *until—*

KRISTINE.
Good evening.

NORA.
Kristine!

TORVALD.
Kristine, why are you here so late?

KRISTINE.
Yeah, sorry, I was just really looking forward to seeing Nora—in her costume.

NORA.
Have you just been sitting here waiting the whole time?

KRISTINE.
Yeah, unfortunately I didn't get here in time. You were already upstairs and I didn't wanna leave before getting to see you.

TORVALD *takes off* **NORA'S** *shawl and spins her around.*

TORVALD.
Yes, take a good look at her. I think she's worth looking at. Isn't she exquisite, Kristine?

KRISTINE.
Yeah, she is.

TORVALD.
Isn't she *exceptionally* exquisite? That was the general consensus at the party, you know. But she's awfully stubborn, this sweet little thing. What're we even supposed to do with her? Would you believe I almost had to drag her out of there?

NORA.
Torvald, you're gonna regret not letting me stay, not even for a half hour.

TORVALD.
[Rambles on happily, slightly drunk] You hear how she talks to me, Kristine? She dances her Tarantella, is a tremendous hit—which was well deserved, by the way—although the performance was maybe a bit *too*

authentic—more so, I mean, than what an artistic representation would usually entail, strictly speaking. But never mind about that! The important thing is, she was a *hit*—a tremendous hit. Should I then just let hang around after that? Dilute the impact? No, thanks!

So I took my little exquisite Capri-girl—my *capricious* little Capri-girl, get it?—on my arm, took one quick lap around the room, a curtsey here, a bow there, and then, as they say in novels, this beautiful vision vanished into thin air. A finale should always be effective, Kristine. But it's impossible for me to get that into her little head. Wow, is it hot in here.

He throws his domino cloak on a chair and opens the door to his office.

Huh! It's all dark in there. Oh, of course—excuse me—.

He goes into his office and lights some candles.

NORA.
[in a hurried and breathless whisper] Well?

KRISTINE.
[in a low voice] I've had a chat with him.

NORA.
And?

KRISTINE.
Nora, you need to tell your husband.

NORA.
[in an expressionless voice] I knew it.

KRISTINE.
You have *nothing* to worry about far as Nils is concerned. But you *have* to tell him.

NORA.
I'm not gonna tell him.

KRISTINE.
Then the letter will.

They stare at each other for a second.

NORA.
Thank you, Kristine. Now I know exactly what I have to do.

TORVALD *saunters back into the living room.*

TORVALD.
Well, Kristine, have you admired her sufficiently?

KRISTINE.
Yes, and now I'll say goodnight.

TORVALD.
Aww, already? By the way, is this yours, the knitting?

*He points to the knitting material sitting out on the table, which **KRISTINE** picks up.*

KRISTINE.
Yeah, thanks, I almost forgot about it.

TORVALD.
So you knit?

KRISTINE.
I do.

TORVALD.
You know what, you should embroider, instead.

KRISTINE.
Really? Why?

TORVALD.
Because it's just so much more beautiful. Let me show you. *[He demonstrates with imaginary materials]* You hold the embroidery like this in your left hand, and use the needle with the right—like this—with a long, delicate curve. Doesn't that look beautiful?

KRISTINE.
Yes, it does—

TORVALD.
But with knitting—it can never be anything except ugly; *[He demonstrates again]* see here—the cramped arms, the knitting-needles going up and down and up and down—almost like playing with chopsticks—. That was some really excellent champagne, by the way.

KRISTINE.
Yeah, well—goodnight, Nora, and stop being so stubborn.

TORVALD.
You said it, Kristine.

KRISTINE.
Goodnight, Mr. Director.

***TORVALD** escorts her to the door.*

TORVALD.
Goodnight, goodnight. You'll get home all right, I hope? I know it's late, and I *would* walk you—but you don't really have that far to go, do you? Goodnight, goodnight.

She leaves. He shuts the door behind her and comes back in.

Finally! I thought she'd never leave. She's so boring, isn't she?

NORA.
Aren't you exhausted, Torvald?

TORVALD.
No, not at all.

NORA.
Sleepy?

TORVALD.
Not one bit. The opposite, actually. I feel totally awake. You?—you look tired *and* sleepy.

NORA.
Yeah, I'm very tired. I wanna go to bed soon.

TORVALD.
There, see? So I was right not to let you stay there long.

NORA.
Yes, everything you do is right, Torvald.

He kisses her forehead.

TORVALD.
Finally, the little goldfinch speaks like a human. *[He smiles at her. She smiles back faintly]* By the way, did you notice how cheerful Rank was tonight?

NORA.
Oh? Was he? I didn't really get a chance to talk to him.

TORVALD.
I barely got a few words in with him myself. Still, it's been a long time since I saw him in this good of a mood.

He looks at her for a bit, one thing clearly on his mind, then comes closer to her.

Hmm, it's so nice to be back home again. To be all alone with you—you adorable little thing!

NORA.
Don't look at me like that, Torvald.

TORVALD.
What, I'm not allowed look at my most prized possession?—at all this glory that's mine and mine alone?

NORA goes to the other side of the table.

NORA.
You shouldn't say things like that to me tonight.

He follows her.

TORVALD.
Looks like you still have the Tarantella in your body. And sweetheart it makes you even more attractive than you already are. Hear that?—the guests are starting to leave. *[In a lower voice.]* Nora—soon, the whole place will be quiet.

NORA.
Yeah, I would sure hope so.

TORVALD.
You do, don't you? You know why I barely talk to you when we're out together out at an event like this? Why I try to stay away from you the whole time?—you wanna know why? It's because I like to pretend that you're my secret lover, and that no one has a clue there's anything going on between us.

NORA.
Oh, yeah, yes…yes—I know you think about me all the time.

TORVALD.
And when we leave, and I get to drape a shawl on your beautiful shoulders—over your delicate back—then I like to pretend that you're my young bride. That we just got home from our wedding and I finally get to carry you inside my home—that I'm alone with you for the first time—all alone with you, my sweet little angel, just like we are now. You were on my mind the entire night. When I watched you captivate and mesmerize the guests with your Tarantella, Nora, I swear it set my whole body on fire. I couldn't take it anymore. That's why I brought you down here so early—

NORA.
Go to sleep, Torvald! I just wanna be alone. I'm not really in the mood—

TORVALD.
[playfully, clearly missing her signals] What's that supposed to mean? Are you trying to be funny, little Nora! Not really in the mood! So I guess I'm not really your husband?

A knock on the front door.

NORA.
[startled] Was that a—?

TORVALD.
[Towards the door] Who is it?

RANK.
[outside] It's me. Can I come in for a second?

TORVALD.
[Softly, resentfully] Oh, what does he want now? *[Aloud.]* Just a minute!

TORVLAD *marches to the front door, unlocks and opens it.*

Rank, it's so nice of you not to pass over our door.

RANK.
I heard your voice and thought I might drop in.

With a cursory glance around the room.

Ah, yes!—these precious, familiar spaces. You've made it all nice and cozy in here, you two.

TORVALD.
Sounds like you were pretty nice and cozy upstairs yourself.

RANK.
Definitely. Why shouldn't I? Why not enjoy everything in this world?—at least as much as you can, and for as long as you can. The wine was exceptional—

TORVALD.
Especially the champagne.

RANK.
You noticed that too? It's almost incredible how many I managed to knock back!

NORA.
Torvald also had a lot of champagne tonight.

RANK.
Did he now?

NORA.
Yes, and he's always so entertaining afterwards.

RANK.
Well, why not enjoy an entertaining evening after a productive day?

TORVALD.
Productive? Unfortunately, that's not a word I can use to describe my day.

RANK.
But I can!

NORA.
Doctor Rank, you must've completed a scientific investigation today.

RANK.
Exactly.

TORVALD.
Well, what do you know!—little Nora's talking about scientific investigations now!

NORA.
[ignoring him] And—should I congratulate you on the results?

RANK.
Yes you should.

NORA.
So it's good news?

RANK.
The best possible for both doctor and patient: *certainty*.

NORA.
[quickly] Certainty?

RANK.
Absolute certainty. So shouldn't I enjoy an entertaining evening after that?

NORA.
Yes, you're right, Doctor Rank.

TORVALD.
I second that! As long as you don't end up paying for it in the morning.

RANK.
Well, you can't have anything in this life without paying for it.

NORA.
Doctor Rank—do you enjoy masquerades?

RANK.
Sure, when there's a whole lot of bizarre costumes around.

NORA.
Tell me—what should the two of us be for the next one?

TORVALD.
You little scatterbrain!—how are you already thinking about the next party?

RANK.
The two of us? Well, let me see. You should go as felicity personified—

TORVALD.
Yeah, and what exactly do you suggest as an appropriate costume for *that*?

RANK.
Just let your wife wear and do exactly what she does every single day—

TORVALD.
How very well said! So then, do you know what you would be?

RANK.
Yes, my good friend, I already have that figured out.

TORVALD.
And?

RANK.
At the next masquerade party I will be invisible.

TORVALD.
That's pretty funny, actually.

RANK.
I would need a big black hat—have you ever heard about the hat of invisibility? If you put it on, no one can see you.

TORVALD.
[suppressing a smile] No, no, you're right.

RANK.
But now to get back to what I really came here for. Torvald, give me a cigar—one of the dark Havanas.

TORVALD.
My pleasure.

He offers him his cigar case. **RANK** *takes one and cuts off the end.*

RANK.
Thanks.

NORA.
Let me give you a light.

*NORA strikes a match and holds it out for **RANK**, who lights his cigar.*

RANK.
Thanks for that. And now goodbye!

TORVALD.
Goodbye, goodbye, my friend!

NORA.
Sleep well, Doctor Rank.

RANK.
Thank you for that wish.

NORA.
Wish me the same.

RANK.
You? Well, if you want me to—sleep well! And thanks for the light.

He nods to them both and leaves.

TORVALD.
[in a subdued voice] He drank way more than he should've.

NORA.
[absently] Maybe.

TORVALD takes his keys out of his pocket and goes out into the foyer.

NORA.
Torvald? What're you doing there?

TORVALD.
Just emptying the mailbox. It's pretty full. There won't be any room to put the morning paper there, otherwise.

NORA.
Are you gonna work tonight?

TORVALD.
You know that I'm not. What's this? Someone tampered with the lock.

NORA.
Tampered with—?

TORVALD.
Yeah, definitely. Why? I wouldn't've thought the maids—. There's a broken hairpin here. Nora, it looks like one of yours—

NORA.
[quickly] It was probably just the kids—

TORVALD.
Then you need to break them out of this habit. There—finally got it open.

He takes out the contents of the mailbox, and calls into the kitchen.

Helena!—Helena, turn off the light in the entrance.

He goes back into the room, closes the door and holds out his hand full of letters, going through them and turning them over while **NORA** *stands by the window.*

Would you look at that—see how much there is? What's this?

NORA.
The letter! Oh no, no, Torvald!

TORVALD.
Two cards—from Rank.

NORA.
From Doctor Rank?

TORVALD.
[looking at them] Doctor Rank, M.D. They were on top. He must've put them in before he left.

NORA.
Is there anything written on them?

TORVALD.
There's a black cross over his name. See? How morbid! It's like he's announcing his own death.

NORA.
That's exactly what he was doing.

TORVALD.
What? Do you know something? What did he tell you?

NORA.
Yeah. He said when the cards arrive, it means he's finally saying his goodbyes to us. He wants to shut himself off and die alone.

TORVALD.
The poor guy! I knew I wasn't gonna have him around for a long time. But this is too soon! And then to just hide himself like a wounded animal!

NORA.
When it has to happen, it's better that it happen quietly—don't you think so, Torvald?

TORVALD.
He was basically part of our family. I can't even picture him gone…It's almost like he'd become a dark cloud casting a shadow on our sunlit happiness. Well, then, maybe it's for the best. For him, at least. And maybe for us too, Nora. Now you and I only have each other to lean on.

He puts his arms around her.

My precious wife, I don't think I can hold you tight enough. You know, Nora—there were a lot of times when I wished that you'd be threatened by something dangerous, so that I could risk life, limb, and everything else for you.

NORA breaks herself free from him, and speaks firmly and emphatically.

NORA.
You should read your letters, Torvald.

TORVALD.
No, no, not tonight. I just wanna be here with you.

NORA.
With the thought of your friend dying—?

TORVALD.
No, you're right, it's affected both of us. Something ugly's come between us, Nora—these thoughts of death and decay. We have to try and free our minds of all that. Until then—we should each stay in separate rooms.

She puts her arms around his neck.

NORA.
Goodnight, Torvald—Goodnight!

He kisses her forehead.

TORVALD.
Goodnight, my little goldfinch. Sleep well.

He takes his letters, goes into his office and closes the door behind him. Wild-eyed, NORA fumbles around, grabs TORVALD'S domino cloak and throws it around herself. She then grabs her shawl and puts it over her head.

NORA.
[in quick, hoarse, irregular whispers] Never see him again. Never. Never. Never. Never see the kids again, either. Not them either. Never. Never— The icy, black water—the bottomless—If only it was all over! He has it now—he's reading it. Oh no, no, not yet. Torvald, goodbye to you and the kids!

As she's about to rush out, **TORVALD** *throws his door open and stands there with a paper in his hand.*

TORVALD.
Nora!

NORA.
[screams out loud] Ah!—

TORVALD.
What is this? Do you know what's in this letter?

NORA.
Yes, I do. Let me go! Let me get out!

TORVALD *grabs her and holds her back. She tries to break free.*

TORVALD.
Where are you going?

NORA.
You can't save me, Torvald!

He stumbles backwards.

TORVALD.
Is this true, what he wrote here? Terrible! No, no—it's impossible. This can't be true.

NORA.
It is true. I have loved you more than anything in the world.

TORVALD.
Oh, don't come to me with dumb excuses.

She takes a step towards him.

NORA.
Torvald—!

TORVALD.
You unfortunate creature—what've you done?

NORA.
Let me go. You shouldn't have to suffer for me. You shouldn't take on this burden alone.

TORVALD.
Enough with the comedy.

He locks the door.

You're gonna stay here and give me an explanation. Do you understand what you've done? Answer me! Do you understand?

She stares at him incessantly, a look of coldness growing in her face.

NORA.
Yes, now I'm beginning to understand completely.

He paces around the room.

TORVALD.
What a horrible awakening! All these eight years—the woman who was my pride and joy—a hypocrite, a liar—worse, worse—a criminal! What a bottomless abyss of ugliness and disgrace!—The shame! Oh, God, the shame!

NORA remains silent, her eyes fixed on him. He stops in front of her.

I should've suspected that something like that would happen. I should've seen it coming. All your father's frivolous ideals—be quiet!—you've inherited all of your father's frivolous ideals. No religion, no morals, no sense of duty—. And now I'm being punished for turning a blind eye to him! I did it for you, and *this* is how you repay me?

NORA.
Yes, this is how.

TORVALD.
Now you have destroyed all my happiness. You've wasted my entire future for me. Oh, God, that's awful to think about! I'm at the mercy of an immoral man. He can do whatever he wants to me, demand anything he wants from me, order and command me however he wants—I wouldn't dare say no. And I'm forced to sink to these miserable lows because of one reckless woman!

NORA.
When I'm gone from this world, you'll be free.

TORVALD.
Oh, please, spare me the fake gestures. Your father always had plenty of those ready. What good would it do me if you were "gone from this world,"

as you say? Not even a little. He can make the whole thing public anyway. And if he does, then I'd be suspected of having been aware of your criminal act. People might even believe that I was behind the whole thing—that I put you up to it! And I have you to thank for all of this—the woman I've lifted up with my own hands throughout our whole marriage. Do you understand now what you've done to me?

NORA.
[with a calm coldness] Yes.

TORVALD.
This is so unbelievable that I can't even understand it. I'll have to try and figure a way out anyway. Take off that shawl. Take it off, now! I have to try and pacify him somehow. This thing must be kept quiet at all costs. And as far as you and I go, we'll have to make it look like nothing's changed between us—only in the eyes of the world. You'll stay in my house, of course. But I won't allow you to raise the kids! I wouldn't risk trusting them to you. That I would have to say this to the woman that I've loved so much, and who I still—. Well, that's all in the past. From now on there's no more talk of happiness. Only of trying to save the remains, the stumps, the façade—

A bell rings in the foyer.

[startled] What's this now? So late! Can the most awful—? Can he—? Hide yourself, Nora. Say you're sick.

NORA *stands motionless.* **TORVALD** *goes and unlocks the door to the foyer.* **HELENA**, *half undressed, steps in and awkwardly tries to ignore the tense, uncomfortable atmosphere.* **TORVLAD** *glares at her while* **NORA** *looks away. She addresses* **NORA** *directly.*

HELENA.
[excessively-formal, with barely-contained annoyance] A letter has arrived for the Mrs.

TORVALD.
Give it to me.

He snatches the letter out of **HELENA'S** *hands. She gives an unsure curtsey and steps back out into the foyer,* **TORVALD** *slamming the door behind her. He stares at the envelope as he walks over to the lamp.*

Yes, it's from him. You won't get it. I'll read it myself.

NORA.
Then read.

TORVALD.
I barely have the nerve to do it. Maybe we're just souls lost in the desert, the both of us. No, I have to know.

He quickly tears open the letter and scans over a few lines, the expression on his face changing. He looks through another paper that was enclosed and cries out joyfully. **NORA** *looks at him inquisitively.*

Nora! Nora!—No, I have to read it one more time—. Yes, yes, it's true! I'm saved! Nora, I'm saved!

NORA.
And me?

TORVALD.
You too, of course! We're both saved, you and I both. Look, he sent you your bond back. He said he regrets and apologizes—that a happy change in his life—oh, who cares about that! We are saved, Nora! Nobody can do anything to you. Oh, Nora, Nora!—no, first I have to destroy this disgusting thing. Let's see—.

He takes a closer look at the bond.

No, no, I don't even wanna look at it. The whole thing will be nothing more than a nightmare to me.

He tears up the bond and both letters, throws them all into the fireplace, and watches them burn.

There—it's all gone. He said that since Christmas Eve you've—. These must've been three awful days for you, Nora.

NORA.
I've been fighting a tough battle the past three days.

TORVALD.
And agonized, and saw no other way out except to—. No, we won't bring up all that ugliness. We'll only celebrate and repeat: "It's over! It's over!" Listen to me, Nora. You don't seem to get it: it is over. What's this?—this stiff expression! Now, poor little Nora, I definitely understand! You don't think you could allow yourself to believe that I really forgive you. But it's true, Nora, I swear to you! I forgive you everything. I know that what you did, you did out of love for me.

NORA.
That is true.

TORVALD.
You have loved me as much as a wife should love her husband. You just lack the insight to judge the proper means to your ends. But do you think you're any less precious to me, just because you don't understand how to act on your own? No, no! You can lean on me. I will advise you. I'll guide you. Actually, I wouldn't even be a man if this helpless femininity didn't make you twice as attractive in my eyes. Don't hold on to the harsh things I said in my initial shock, when I thought everything was going to collapse in on me. I forgive you, Nora! I swear to you that I forgive you.

NORA.
Thank you for your forgiveness.

She goes to the bedroom.

TORVALD.
No, stay—. *[Looks in.]* What're you doing in the alcove?

NORA.
[off] Taking off my costume.

He stands by the open door.

TORVALD.
Yes, okay, you do that. And try to calm down and regain your composure, my terrified little goldfinch. Rest easy now; I'll keep you safe under my wings.

He paces up and down by the door.

How warm and cozy is our home, Nora? This is your shelter. This is where I'll keep you safe, like a hunted dove I rescued from the claws of a vicious hawk.

It'll happen, little by little, sweetheart, believe me. Tomorrow everything will seem totally different to you. Soon it'll all be back to the way things were. Before you know it, I won't even have to keep reminding you that I've forgiven you; you yourself will know it in your heart.

How can you think it would even occur to me to reject you, or even blame you for anything? You have no idea what a real man's heart is like, Nora. For a man, there's something so indescribably sweet and satisfying in knowing that he has forgiven his wife—forgiven her truly, and with all his heart.

She then, in a way, belongs to him twice; he's given her a whole new life, if you will; and she has, in a sense, become both his wife and his child. And that's what you'll be to me after this, you confused, helpless little thing.

Don't you worry about a thing, Nora! Just be open and honest with me, and I will serve as your conscience and your guide—. What're you doing, not going to bed? You put on a new outfit?

NORA steps out in her everyday clothes.

NORA.
Yes, Torvald, I put on a new outfit.

TORVALD.
But why now, this late—?

NORA.
I won't be sleeping tonight.

TORVALD.
But, sweetheart—

She checks her watch.

NORA.
It's not so late yet. Sit down, Torvald. You and I have a lot to talk about.

She sits down at one side of the table.

TORVALD.
Nora—what is this?—this stiff expression again?

NORA.
Sit down. It's gonna take some time. I have a lot to talk to you about.

He sits down at the opposite side of the table.

TORVALD.
You're scaring me, Nora!—and I don't understand you.

NORA.
No, that's just it. You *don't* understand me, and I've never understood you, either—until tonight. No, don't interrupt me. You're just gonna listen to what I have to say. It's our day of reckoning, Torvald.

TORVALD.
What do you mean by that?

She contemplates silently for a short moment.

NORA.
Isn't there one thing that seems off to you when we're sitting here like this?

TORVALD.
What would that be?

NORA.
We've been married for eight years now. Do you realize this is the first time that the two of us, you and me, husband and wife, have had a serious conversation?

TORVALD.
Serious conver—? What does that mean?

NORA.
For eight consecutive years—no, longer than that—from the very beginning of our relationship, we have never said a single serious thing to each other about a single serious subject.

TORVALD.
Was I supposed to constantly talk to you about worries that you wouldn't've been able to help me with anyway?

NORA.
I'm not talking about worries. I'm saying that we've never really sat down together to try and get to the bottom of anything.

TORVALD.
But, Nora, sweetheart, would that have even been appropriate for you?

NORA.
And there you have it; you've never understood me. I've been mistreated, Torvald—first by dad and then by you.

TORVALD.
What?! By us?—by *us*, who have loved you more than anyone else in the world?

NORA.
[shaking her head] You never loved me. You only loved the idea of being in love with me.

TORVALD.
Nora, are you even listening to what's coming out of your mouth?

NORA.
It's absolutely true, Torvald. When I was at home with dad, he told me his opinions about everything, and so I formed the same opinions. And if I had other ones, I kept them to myself, because he wouldn't've liked it. He called me his baby doll, and he treated me the same way I would treat my dolls. And then I came to your house—

TORVALD.
Is that what you call getting married?

NORA.
[undisturbed] —I mean that I was simply passed from dad's hands into yours. You arranged everything according to your own tastes, and so I acquired the same tastes as you—or at least I pretended to, I'm not sure really—I think it's both, sometimes one, sometimes the other. When I look back on it, it seems to me that I had been living here like a beggar—just hand to mouth. I existed only to perform tricks for you, Torvald. But that's how you wanted it. You and dad have committed a great sin against me. It's your fault that I've made nothing of myself.

TORVALD.
Nora, how ridiculous and ungrateful of you! Haven't you been happy here?

NORA.
No, I've never been happy. I thought I was, but I've never been.

TORVALD.
Not—not happy?

NORA.
No, just glad. And you've always been so kind to me. But our home's been nothing more than a playroom. I've been your wife-doll, just like at home I was dad's baby doll, and here the kids have been my dolls. I thought it was fun when you played with me, just like they think it's fun when I play with them. That's what our marriage's been like, Torvald.

TORVALD.
There's some truth to that—regardless of how exaggerated and hysterical it may be. But moving forward, it'll be different. Playtime's over. Now's the time for education.

NORA.
Whose education? Mine, or the kids?

TORVALD.
Both yours and the kids, sweetheart.

NORA.
Sadly, Torvald, you're not the man to educate me on how to be a proper wife for you.

TORVALD.
How can you even say that!

NORA.
And I—how am I even prepared to raise the kids?

TORVALD.
Nora!

NORA.
Didn't you say so yourself a minute ago—that you wouldn't risk trusting me to raise them?

TORVALD.
In a moment of anger! Why would you even take that seriously?

NORA.
Yes, but you were still right. I'm not up to the task. There's another one I have to take on first. I have to try and educate myself—you're not the man to help me with that. I have to do it for myself. And that's why I'm leaving you now.

TORVALD.
[jumps up] What did you just say?

NORA.
I need to be completely alone if I wanna understand myself and everything around me. That's why I can't stay with you anymore.

TORVALD.
Nora, Nora!

NORA.
I'll be leaving immediately. I'm sure Kristine can take me in for the night—

TORVALD.
You're insane! I won't allow it! I forbid you!

NORA.
You can't forbid me anything anymore. I'll only take with me what belongs to me. I won't take anything from you, not now, not ever.

TORVALD.
What sort of insanity is this!

NORA.
Tomorrow I'm going home—I mean, to my old home. It'll be easier for me to find something to do there.

TORVALD.
You're just a blind, inexperienced thing!

NORA.
I have to go out and *get* experience, Torvald.

TORVALD.
To leave your home, your husband and your kids! And you don't even consider what people will say!

NORA.
I can't take that into account. I only know what's right for me.

TORVALD.
Oh, that's outrageous. And so you'd neglect your most sacred duties?

NORA.
What, exactly, do you consider my most sacred duties?

TORVALD.
Of course *I* need to tell you that! Aren't they your duties to your husband and your kids?

NORA.
I have other duties that're just as sacred.

TORVALD.
You do not. What duties would *those* be?

NORA.
The ones to myself.

TORVALD.
You are first and foremost a wife and a mother.

NORA.
I don't believe that anymore. I believe that I am first and foremost a human being, just as much as you are—or, at the very least, that I should try to be. I know, of course, that most people would agree with you, Torvald, and that those views are found in books. But I can't settle for what most people say, or what's found in books. I have to think these things through for myself and get to understand them.

TORVALD.
Don't you understand your place in your own home? Don't you have a reliable guide for these things?—Don't you have a *religion*?

NORA.
Oh, Torvald, I don't even know what religion really is.

TORVALD.
What are you saying?

NORA.
I don't know anything more than what Reverend Hansen said when I was

getting ready for my confirmation. He told me that religion was *this* and *that*. When I get away from all of this, and I'm on my own, I'll have to look more into that, too. I wanna see if it's right, what Reverend Hansen said, or at least if it's right for *me*.

TORVALD.
This is unheard of for a girl your age! But if religion can't set you straight, then let me at least see if you have some conscience. I assume you have *some* moral sense? Or—tell me—maybe you don't have any?

NORA.
Yeah, Torvald, that's not an easy question to answer. I really don't know that, either. I'm pretty confused about these things. I only know that I have a very different opinion on this than you. I also hear that the laws are not at all what I had thought. But for them to be considered *fair*, that I can't wrap my head around. So a woman doesn't have the right to spare her old, dying father, or even to save her husband's life? I don't believe in that.

TORVALD.
You talk like a child. You don't understand the society you live in.

NORA.
No, I don't. But now I wanna try. I have to find out who's right, society or me.

TORVALD.
You're sick, Nora! You have a fever. I almost think you're completely out of your mind.

NORA.
I've never felt as clear and confident as I do now.

TORVALD.
And you're clear and confident about leaving your husband and your kids?

NORA.
Yes, I am.

TORVALD.
Then there's only *one* possible explanation.

NORA.
What?

TORVALD.
You don't love me anymore.

NORA.
Well, yeah, that's exactly it.

TORVALD.
Nora!—how can you even say that?

NORA.
Believe me, it hurts me so much, Torvald, because you've always been so kind to me. But I can't do anything about it. I don't love you anymore.

TORVALD.
[regaining his composure] Are you clear and confident about that, too?

NORA.
Yes, perfectly clear and confident. That's why I don't wanna be here anymore.

TORVALD.
And can you explain to me exactly how I lost your love?

NORA.
Yes, I can. It was tonight, when the Divine didn't happen, because then I saw that you weren't the man I had imagined.

TORVALD.
The Divine?! Explain yourself more clearly. I really don't understand you at all.

NORA.
I've waited so patiently for eight years now, because, my God, I realized that the Divine doesn't just happen in everyday life. Then this horrible disaster fell on me, and I felt so incredibly sure: the Divine is finally happening now. When Nils' letter was out there, it never even crossed my mind that you'd just accept his demands. I was so incredibly sure that, instead, you'd say to him: make this public for the whole world to see. And then when he did—

TORVALD.
Yeah, go on? What happens in this scenario after I freely offer up my wife to be disgraced—?

NORA.
And then when he did, I was so incredibly sure you'd come forward to take the blame for everything, and say that you're the guilty one.

TORVALD.
Nora—!

NORA.
You're probably thinking that I'd never let you sacrifice yourself like that for me. Of course I wouldn't. But then here's the dilemma: what weight would my words have carried against yours? No one would've believed me, and you would've needlessly suffered because of what I was sure had been your endless love for me. *That* was the Divine that I had nervously hoped for, and preventing it was why I wanted to end my life.

TORVALD.
I would've been more than glad to work day and night for you, Nora—suffer through pain and hardships for you. But no man would sacrifice his *honor* for the one he loves.

NORA.
Hundreds of thousands of women have done that.

TORVALD.
You think and talk like a child.

NORA.
Maybe. But you don't think and talk like the man I would want to share my life with. As soon as your fear was over—not fear of what threatened *me*, but of what might've happened to *you*—when the whole danger was over—then for you it was like nothing had happened at all. Just like before, I was your little goldfinch, your doll, which you now had to handle twice as gently, since she was so fragile and weak. Torvald—it was then it dawned on me that, for eight years I had been living here with a total stranger, and that I'd given him three children—. I can't even think about it or I'd tear myself apart!

TORVALD.
[sadly] I see it, I do see it. There's definitely an abyss that has come between us. But, Nora, don't you think it's possible to fill it back up?

NORA.
The way I am now, I can't be a wife to you anymore.

TORVALD.
I have the strength to become a different man.

NORA.
Maybe—if your doll's taken away from you.

TORVALD.
But to be separate!—to separate from you! No, no, Nora, I can't even imagine.

She goes out into the foyer and comes back with her coat, hat and a small bag, which she sets on a chair by the table.

NORA.
That makes it all the more inevitable.

TORVALD.
Nora, Nora, not now! Wait until tomorrow.

She puts on her coat.

NORA.
I can't spend the night in a strange man's house.

TORVALD.
But can't we live here like brother and sister—?

She puts on her hat.

NORA.
[laughing sadly] You know very well that wouldn't last long.

She wraps the shawl around her shoulders.

Goodbye, Torvald. I don't wanna see the kids. I know they're in better hands than mine. The way I am now, I can't be anything to them.

TORVALD.
But some day, Nora—some day?

NORA.
How would I know? I don't even have a clue what'll happen to me.

TORVALD.
But you're my wife, now and regardless of what happens.

NORA.
Listen, Torvald. When a wife leaves her husband's house, like I'm doing now, I've heard that by law he is released from any and all obligations to her. In any case, I release you from any obligation. You shouldn't feel committed to anything, and neither should I. There must be full freedom on both sides. Look, here's your ring back. Give me mine.

TORVALD.
That too?

NORA.
That too.

TORVALD.
Here.

They exchange rings.

NORA.
Well. Yes, now it's all over. I'm leaving the keys here. The maids know everything that needs to be done around the house—better than I do. Tomorrow, after I've left town, Kristine will come here to pack up my own things that I brought with me from home. I will send for them.

TORVALD.
All over. All over!—Nora, will you never think of me again?

NORA.
I know that I'll often think of you, the children, and this house.

TORVALD.
Can I write to you?

NORA.
No—never. You're not allowed to do that.

TORVALD.
But at least let me send you—

NORA.
Nothing—nothing—

TORVALD.
—help you if you need it.

NORA.
No, don't—I don't accept anything from strangers.

TORVALD.
Nora—can I *never* be anything more than a stranger to you?

She picks up her bag.

NORA.
Oh, Torvald, that would require the most Divine thing of all.

TORVALD.
Name this most Divine thing!

NORA.
Both you and I would have to change so much that—. Torvald, I don't believe in anything divine anymore.

TORVALD.
But I want to believe. Tell me! Change so much that—?

NORA.
That our coexistence would become a real marriage. Goodbye.

She walks out through the foyer. **TORVALD** *sinks down on a chair and buries his face in his hands*

TORVALD.
Nora! Nora!

He looks around the room and stands up.

Empty. She's not here anymore.

A hope flashes across his face.

The most Divine thing of all —?

The sound of the street-door slamming shut is heard from below.

END

Printed in Great Britain
by Amazon